Bloodlines of Revolution

Ayla Jones

Book Cover by TMT Cover Designs

Editing by Kate Seger

The header illustration by Dom Sabasti (Midjourney)

1st edition 2023

Acknowledgements

I wish to thank Kate Seger for her exceptional editorial skills, keen insight, and tireless efforts in refining this narrative. Your contributions have enhanced the story immeasurably. am deeply indebted to TMT Cover Design for the stunning covers for the series and also Dom Sabasti's talent for the bat illustration. Your creative vision, skill, and passion have added depth and beaty to these pages.

I'd like to dedicate this story to my family.

Contents

Chapter One

The Last Day Alive

On Christmas Eve, Henri D'Ardent's world crumbled. The French Revolution, once a distant rumble, had come to his doorstep, bearing a deadly reckoning. It was the last time Henri saw himself alive—or alive as a human. "How did it come to this?" Henri wondered, his thoughts spiraling into the past, seeking answers in the events that had brought him to this precipice.

Since July 1789, the French Revolution had ravaged the nation, leaving a trail of blood and destruction in its wake. The once-mighty Bourbon monarchy had fallen, and with it, the very fabric of French society. The gruesome executions of King Louis XVI in January 1793 and Queen Marie Antoinette in October of the same year sent shockwaves throughout the land, striking fear into the hearts of the aristocracy.

Henri's parents, Jean and Marie D'Ardent, left for England to escape all this chaos, but Henri still did not want to leave. "Why should I leave my home and my country?"

"It's not safe here," his father told him, but Henri shook his head.

"No, I will stay here. I don't believe they will come here. It's just Paris and the more famous noble families the Jacobins are after." Henri looked stern.

"As you wish. I will take your mother with me, and we hope you will stay safe." Jean paused, his voice heavy with emotion. "Remember, our family's legacy is not tied to this land alone. We will rebuild, wherever we may be."

The farewell was bittersweet, the weight of uncertainty hanging in the air. Henri's parents departed with a small contingent of loyal servants, carrying a fraction of their valuables. The hidden safe, concealed behind a portrait of Henri's ancestors, held the remainder of their wealth.

After saying goodbyes, they left with some of their valuables leaving Henri some in the hidden safe.

The alarming reports of decapitations, imprisonments, and massacres spread like wildfire, prompting many aristocrats to flee for their lives. England, with its promise of refuge and safety, beckoned. Yet, Henri remained resolute, refusing to abandon his homeland.

At first, Henri had doubted the horrific tales of the Revolution's brutality. He couldn't fathom that his countrymen, once renowned for their elegance and civility, could commit such atrocities. But as the months passed and the body count rose, he realized the terrible truth.

The Reign of Terror had unleashed a frenzy of class hatred, targeting the nobility with merciless ferocity. The fall of the royal family had set a chilling precedent: if the king and queen were not spared, no aristocrat would be safe. The very fact that Henri still bore the title of Count made him a prime target for the Revolutionaries.

As panic spread, Henri's neighbors, the Escargots, had packed lightly and fled. They offered him a place in their four-wheel horse-driven carriage, but Henri declined. The Escargots' usually stately demeanor was replaced by urgency, each family member clutching a single, modest satchel containing only the most essential personal items. Their sprawling estate, once filled with laughter and life, stood vacant.

"Please, come with us. It's not safe for any of us aristocrats in France." Count Escargot tried to convince him to leave, but Henri vehemently refused. Count Escargot added, "I will try to go to England with my family. We aren't taking much with us. If you change your mind, you know where to find us." And they drove away in haste.

Despite the urgent warnings from friends and other upper-class families, Henri hesitated, torn between loyalty to his heritage and the danger stalking him. Henri's sense of duty and nostalgia for the France he once knew kept him rooted, even as the ground beneath him crumbled.

As the days shortened and days got shorter during late fall and when the winter's chill finally set in, Henri's resolve began to waver. Should he have gone with his parents?

The knock on the door, the whispered warning, or the sudden appearance of Revolutionary guards could come at any moment. He realized his time was running out. He did not know what to do... Would he join his parents and the ranks of the fugitive aristocrats in England, or would he face the increasingly likely prospect of imprisonment, trial, and guillotine?

He did not even know if his parents managed to cross the canal to England. He had not received any letters from them.

*And then today happened...*What he remembered was spotty, and incoherent, and even now it felt like it was just a nightmare.

The Early Morning Visitors on Christmas

The early morning air was shattered by the clatter of horses' hooves and the murmur of menacing voices.

Henri rushed to the window, his heart racing, and peered into the darkness. The flickering torches below cast eerie shadows on the faces of the sans-culottes, their distinctive striped pants a badge of revolutionary fervor.

"Mon Dieu, no!" Henri cursed, recognizing the Jacobins, the radical zealots who had taken over the Revolution. He quickly put on his pants and shirt, but he was too late to escape.

A loud crack told him that the front door was kicked open. And he rushed to the staircase to view downstairs and saw the intruders storming in, their boots thundering on the wooden floor. Henri tried to protest, but his words were lost in chaos. The Jacobins seized him, their rough hands tearing him from his home.

Henri clung to the doorframe, his knuckles white, as the men wrenched him away. "You cannot do this! I haven't done anything!" he shouted.

The leader, a burly man with a scar on his left cheek, sneered. "You're a count, D'Ardent. Your kind is finished. The people have risen."

Henri's eyes blazed with fury. "This is madness, it will pass. I will return."

A blow from behind sent Henri crashing to the ground, and everything went dark.

In Paris

When he regained consciousness, Henri found himself in an open carriage, surrounded by wooden bars and the anxious faces of fellow aristocrats. The vehicle rattled through Paris's crowded streets, with onlookers jeering, spitting, and hurling mud at them.

A young revolutionary, his eyes aglow with fanaticism, spat at Henri through the bars. "Vive la Révolution!"

"What is this?" Henri whispered.

The man next to him replied, sighing. "We are a spectacle – the imprisoned aristocrats. The streets of

Paris are filled with spectators; it is always an event here when the prison transportation comes through." He stared at Henri. " The Jacobins always arrange a visible transportation through the streets, signifying the authority of the new regime and their power, and acting as a deterrent against potential uprisings." He glanced around and noticed the armed guards following them. "However, they don't want us to be killed before the mock trial."

"I'm in Paris," Henri repeated. *This was not good.*

The streets were filled with Commoners wearing the tricolor; red, blue, and white, originating from the King's colors—white royal flag—and the City of Paris— red and blue. Women and officers wore the tricolor cockade on their headpieces, whereas many men wore the red Phrygian cap with a French tricolor cockade on the front to symbolize their support of the Revolution. When the prison transportation drove through the crowd, the people threw rotten tomatoes and stones toward it and chanted, "Kill the king. Kill the queen. Kill the aristocrats." It was worse than he had imagined.

Henri slumped against the wooden beams of the carriage's wall, cradling his throbbing head. Would he face the guillotine's deadly kiss? Or would reason prevail?

As the vehicle jostled onward, Henri whispered a desperate prayer. "God protect us, and France, forgive them, for they know not what they do."

The carriage finally halted before a stone building.

"No, not the Tribunal," one of the ladies whispered, eyes wide in horror.

Henri's stomach churned when he heard the words – the Tribunal was the 'court' sentencing all the aristocrats. When the locked door was opened, he among the other aristocrats was dragged into the Committee of Public Safety's Tribunal – a kangaroo court, not a sanctuary of justice.

This was no ordinary courtroom. The room pulsed with the fervor of a war cabinet, where life and death decisions were made with ruthless efficiency. The very air reeked of revolutionary fervor, and Henri knew his fate hung precariously in the balance.

Robespierre, the Incorruptible, presided over the tribunal, his eyes cold and unyielding. "Count Henri D'Ardent, you are accused of counter-revolutionary activities..."

Henri's heart sank. He knew the verdict before the trial began.

The Sentencing

The cold, dimly lit chamber deep within the Revolutionary Tribunal's headquarters seemed to suffocate the very air from Henri D'Ardent's lungs. The walls, once adorned with a royal crest, now bore the stark, blood-red insignia of the Committee of Public Safety.

Henri stood before the raised platform, flanked by two grim-faced guards. Before him, a row of stern judges, their faces chiseled from years of fanaticism, scrutinized him with an unyielding gaze.

At the center of the tribunal, Maximilien Robespierre, the Incorruptible, presided with an air of calculated intensity. His piercing eyes seemed to bore into Henri's very soul.

To Robespierre's right sat Georges Danton, his voice like thunder, and to his left, Louis Antoine de Saint-Just, the Angel of Death, whose youthful face belied his ruthless ideology.

"Count Henri D'Ardent," Robespierre's voice dripped with malice, "you are accused of counter-revolutionary activities, of conspiring against the Republic, and of harboring royalist sympathies."

Henri's voice trembled. "I am innocent. My family has served France for generations."

Danton snarled. "Your family's privilege is precisely the problem. The people will no longer be shackled by aristocratic tyranny."

Saint-Just's voice was silky smooth. "Your wealth, your title, these are crimes against the Revolution. The people demand justice."

The judges conferenced in hushed tones, their faces unreadable.

Henri knew his fate hung by a thread.

Robespierre's gaze snapped back to Henri. "The Tribunal has heard sufficient evidence. The Revolution shows no mercy."

Henri's heart sank. He knew the verdict before the trial began.

As the president lifted his gaze to meet Henri's, he knew the result even before he said it aloud. "The Verdict: Guilty."

Gasping, Henri's knees buckled, and he heard the next words, "The Sentence: Death by guillotine."

The guards dragged him away, his pleas for mercy lost in the crowd's cheering.

No wonder, they were called the Reign of Terror, he thought as he was dragged away. Their reign had claimed another victim.

He struggled to get away, but he was hit again on the back of his head and everything blurred.

The Bastille

And next what he remembered was when he woke up in a dark dungeon, lying on the straw bed, the rats scattered along the floor tiles, a tiny window above him with bars on it. He stood up and tried to look outside, but the window was too high. But from the crowd chanting outside, "Heads off! Take them to the guillotine!" he guessed he had been taken to the Bastille, the infamous prison where they kept the aristocrats before taking them to be beheaded by the guillotine.

Henri knew he had no hope. *No way to survive. What a Christmas. I should have left a long time ago,* he contemplated his destiny. Stubborn to stay and believing he would stay alive and outside the reach of the Jacobins had been a fool's hope.

The daylight faded as the sun set and night arrived. Henri prayed. He hoped that the miracle of Christmas would happen.

The prison grew darker and darker, the cold and pale moonlight the only light in his cell.

He sat on the cold stone floor, leaning against the wall. The guard came by and opened a small slot in the thick wooden door. "You will face your creator tomorrow." The guard cackled and tossed a metal plate with rotten food and some rice on it. "Eat the same food you let us commoners eat," the guard said with a menacing voice. "You and the other members of the noble families will face our lady Guillotine when the sun rises." Then, the guard closed the window again.

Henri buried his face in his hands. He would be killed on Christmas Day. He touched his hair that reached on his shoulders. Soon, the commoners would cut it before beheading him.

And then, like a Christmas wish, Henri heard a voice, "Would you like to live forever?"

Henri turned his head and tried to figure out who spoke and from where.

Chapter Two

The Surprise Visit on Christmas Eve

*T*he voice came from above, Henri D'Ardent thought, craning his neck and trying to see who it was. It was hard to see anything in the dim moonlight, but he saw a shadow moving.

A bat?

Why would a bat fly to prison?

The bat flew in, circled his head, and said, "Filthy here. Nothing like what an aristocrat like you is used to, I bet."

A bat who can talk? But bats can't talk! Henri still didn't believe his senses. He must be hallucinating. Perhaps the hit to his head caused him to see and hear things that did not exist. He raised his hand and touched the sore bump on the back of his skull, and his hand felt wet. *Bloody,* he thought. A head wound like this could be serious.

The bat sat on the ground beside Henri and closed his leathery wings. "You think you are seeing things. So did many of your colleagues in the next cells. Some accepted my offer, and some did not. It's all up to you. Do you want to stay here and die tomorrow, or do you want to come with me and live forever?"

"Who or what are you?" Henri asked.

The bat morphed before him into a gorgeous woman in her twenties. She had curly, long black hair, plump lips, and a curvy figure, and she wore a gauzy cotton gown with long lacy sleeves and a wide lacy neckline that left her round shoulders free and gave a hint of her bountiful breasts.

The minute Henri saw this demon—or that's what he thought this beautiful creature was—he jumped up from the cold floor and quickly attacked it. His hand tightened around the young woman's neck as he slammed her against the stone wall.

The woman choked. She had not expected Henri to attack.

"Go away, demon!" Henri snarled into her ear.

The woman turned her eyes to him and easily pulled his hand away from her throat. She was stronger than Henri, which was surprising. "I'm not a demon," she replied, and her laughter sounded like tiny bells tinkling.

"What are you then?" Henri replied and took a step back.

She stood there, tilting her head, and replied, "I'm a vampire."

"A vampire?" Henri repeated. He backed away from the creature until he felt the wall behind his back. She followed and put her hands on Henri's chest. Henri couldn't go anywhere. The confined space was small, and there was no place to run or hide.

"A vampire," the woman repeated. "You don't know what that is, do you?"

She was so close that Henri could smell her hair—honey and cinnamon-scented.

Henri sighed. He had nothing to lose. "Fine, I am listening. Speak."

She leaned closer and tilted her head back to see Henri's eyes. "A vampire is someone who can live forever. All vampires used to be humans. We don't tolerate the sunlight well, but we thrive in the nighttime."

That doesn't sound awful at all, Henri thought. His eyes moved slowly from her deep, dark eyes to her sawn-like neck and followed the neckline to the shadow between her breasts. Without thinking, Henri moved his hands to her waist and let them rest there. She seemed to fit perfectly in his arms. She was a head shorter than Henri was, and when she stood close to him like this, the top of her head reached his chin.

"What is a vampire?" Henri asked, holding the woman close to him. He still was not sure if he was dreaming. How could he possibly have his arms around a flesh-and-blood woman in his prison cell? He must be dreaming!

"The living dead, some say," the woman replied. ". I've been called a devil too." She laughed again. Then her face turned serious, and she said, "It's a different form of existence. Not mortal, but a reality that diverges from your familiar life. You will be immortal. Like me, you'll discover the ancient art of metamorphosis to a bat, unfolding wings to take to the night skies, though not all of our kind possess this gift. As the sun's warmth yields to the moon's silvery glow, you'll embrace the shadows, your existence woven into the fabric of the night. And as the world around you evolves, you'll adapt and witness generations rise and fall like the stars in the sky."

"That's not too bad compared to the death sentencing I've received," Henri said. "I will be taken to the guillotine tomorrow with other aristocrats. This is my last day alive." His voice broke at the end of the sentence when he realized how close his demise was.

Now, this woman said he could live... Henri latched his gaze on her dark eyes and asked, "Tell me more. First, what is your name? Where do you come from?"

"Call me Joliette," she replied. "I don't have time to tell you everything now. I must get you ready to leave before the guards come. The night goes fast. I can't stay here when the sun rises, nor can you. You need to look dead when the guards arrive for your own good. They won't behead a corpse. You will be dumped into the pile of bodies. You'll have to stay under the bodies until the sun sets. Then you can leave." She stared at Henri and repeated, "It is crucial that you don't leave and expose yourself to sunlight. Stay under the bodies. You won't die there."

"Will you come and find me?" Henri asked, his hands tightening around her tiny waist.

"Someone will come. I don't know if it will be me or someone I know. We are in a hurry to save as many aristocrats as possible. We don't have many hours to do that. Nights are short when dozens of men and women are imprisoned for no other reason than their heritage." She lifted her chin and asked, "Are you ready?"

Henri swallowed. *Am I ready?* he thought. *No, I'm not ready. I'm not ready to die. I'm not ready to be a vampire. I don't want any change. I loved my life as it was. I want it back, but I know I won't. The world has changed, and this is my only chance to see how it changes.*

"Yes," Henri replied.

Chapter Three

Vampire Joliette

"Then let's begin." Joliette pulled Henri's head lower. The moonlight hit the sharp white canines a second before they bit Henri's neck. Henri coiled and tried to push her away, but she was strong and held his head between her hands in an iron grip so that Henri could not move or get away from her. She pressed her luscious body against his, and he felt arousal.

Next, Henri felt dizzy, and then his knees buckled. Joliette held him, her mouth pressed tight on his neck.

Henri opened his eyes and saw the moon and the stars through the bars of the small prison window, and that was the last thing he saw before he passed out.

Joliette lowered her victim down on the cold stone floor, laid on top of him, and finished what she had come there for—sucked almost all the blood out of him, leaving only so little that he lived, not as a human, but as a vampire.

After Joliette had quenched her hunger, she stood up. A few drops of blood dripped down her chin. Joliette looked down at her victim and smiled. She wiped her mouth with the back of her hand, lifted her arms wide, and spiraled around, becoming smaller and smaller until she turned back into a bat. She flapped her leathery black wings and flew up and through the bars of the prison cell's window to the indigo-blue night sky.

She headed to the next cell. You never knew who else would want to transform into a vampire instead of being beheaded. She was sure she could convince more aristocrats to become vampires that night. Their coven would grow, but that would be good. They had plenty of people in this city, and she had also planned to travel and see other countries, perhaps even go across the sea to the new land—America, it was called. She didn't know if there were any vampires there, but she would not mind starting a new coven in a new country. Paris was a sad place now. No more parties in castles, no more lavish dresses and jewelry. The revolution changed everything. Now, people preferred simple clothes, and everyone suspected of siding with the aristocrats was in danger. She had heard that many noble families fled to England. She would like to visit London too. The court and the societal balls might be worth investigating, she considered as she zoomed to the next occupied cell with a lone woman sitting and crying in there.

Joliette sat by the window and studied her before asking, "Would you like to live forever?"

The woman turned her puffy eyes and tear-strike cheeks to her and asked, "Who said that?"

Joliette flew in through the window bars and made the same offer to the young woman as she had done to Henri. She was the third of her victims that night. She was busy because night hours went by fast, and persuading each victim took longer than expected.

By sunrise, Joliette had transformed eight humans into vampires. *Busy night,* she thought and yawned. *Time to go rest.* She flew to the catacombs where her coven was residing. They were underground cemeteries for the city of Paris and accessible through the former Tombe-Issoire mines under the plain of Montrouge. A perfect place for vampires to rest because hardly any humans visited the site during the daytime.

She would spend her daytime there resting. She was full of blood and tired. *I will have to send someone to pick up the new vampires and show them the ropes,* she thought.

Chapter Four

Vampire Joliette's Hideout

J oliette flew through the catacombs until she found a round opening, and there she landed and swiftly transformed back into her human form.

The air was musty.

A few torches were lit here and there and mounted on the stone walls. Caverns on the walls had skeletons in them; some had piled bones, others full skeletons, and some only had skulls. For someone walking here for the first time, it was an eerie sight to see several human skulls and their empty sockets staring from the wall grottos to the visitors. The mice and rats ran discreetly by the walls and hid in the shadows. They had gotten used to the vampire visitors and knew that they were not the ones to bite because they would bite back and kill.

The catacomb was created as a series of interconnected rooms. Some were finished, and some were partially complete. The different levels of the catacomb were about three to eight feet tall, so in some places, Joliette had to crouch or fly as a bat again to move forward faster. The floor was stone and dirt in some areas. She knew that the city of Paris wanted to accommodate more burial places for the dead, and thus, the catacombs were sprawling underground. She had seen the start of the project, and now she could see the different levels of burial sites. All this worked well for her because the more people were buried there, the larger area there was for them to hide, and also, if the grave diggers ever saw them, they would get scared and think that they had awakened the ghosts.

When the ceiling was again higher, Joliette walked briskly ahead, turning first left and right. Then, she walked ahead until she reached another large grotto, where she found twenty other vampires of her coven waiting for her. Some were sitting, and others were standing or pacing impatiently. They knew where she had been and were worried because it was already dawn, and she had not returned.

Joliette exhaled a weary sigh. She had cut it perilously close to sunrise, but she'd survived, and hopefully, her newly turned vampires would too. As the elder of the coven and their creator, she bore the weight of responsibility for their existence. Her clan members, comprised of noblemen and distant relatives of royalty, relied on her for guidance and protection. While she held them in esteem, a lingering fear also gripped her heart – the daunting prospect of what would become of them if she were to fall.

The Revolution's wrath had ravaged the noble families' estates, seeking to eradicate any remaining signs of aristocracy. Joliette's coven, comprised of transformed vampires from these illustrious families, now faced a harsh reality. Their lavish lifestyles were a relic of the past, as safety became their paramount concern.

Living openly in France was impossible. The Commoners and Jacobins hunted them relentlessly, driven by hatred and suspicion. Even if they managed to evade detection, the peasants surrounding their former castles would grow wary of their unnatural vitality and timeless appearance.

Joliette knew they had to flee. In a new land, they could reinvent themselves as reclusive nobles, their eccentricities chalked up to wealth and privilege. No one would suspect their true nature. But staying in France meant constant danger, their very existence threatened by the Revolution's unforgiving fervor.

A new life awaited, one where they could reside in comfortable anonymity, free from the weight of their noble past. Joliette's resolve hardened: it was time to leave France behind and forge a new future, shrouded in secrecy and protected by distance.

"Greetings, beloved ones," Joliette offered, her smile radiating warmth.

"Moon's blessings," her coven members mumbled back.

"Did you find any new members to our coven?" a pale, dark-haired man asked. He wore an expensive gold-decorated suit and multiple jeweled rings on his fingers.

"Yes, Armand, I found eight who wanted to live and not be executed," Joliette replied and added, "I instructed them to pretend to be dead, slow down their breathing, and hide under the pile of bodies when the guards throw them out of their cells. I warned them about the sunshine, and I hope they remember that,"

For new vampires, it was sometimes difficult to obey orders. Joliette remembered how she had lost a couple of new vampires just last week because they thought they could just get up and walk away when their bodies were carried out. They screamed and burned in the bright sunshine. *Sometimes noblemen are stupid,* Joliette thought. *They think they know everything and don't listen to any advice.*

Joliette brushed her long hair back behind her shoulders. Her skin was luminous even in the darkness of the chamber. She knew she was beautiful because she had been bitten when she was barely twenty years old. She had grown up in a wealthy family and had learned how to access more gold and jewelry during her lifetime. The accommodation in the catacombs was not pleasing but at least they were not at the mercy of the revolution forces. If they would find them, they would die – one way or the other.

Several chairs and a table were brought into the chamber for the vampires to sit.

Joliette took one chair and sat down. Sighing, she said, "We'll be busy tonight. We have to pick up our fledglings from the Bastille and bring them here. They will not be able to fly immediately as we can, so we need to be patient with them." She looked around and asked, "Who would like to accompany me to the Bastille?"

As the head of the coven, Joliette could have ordered her coven members to join her on this trip, but she did not want to do that because she knew that some of them had been imprisoned there and had nightmares of the guards and the place. Patiently, she waited for the coven members to decide.

Armand said, "I will come."

Joliette nodded and waited for another answer.

An elderly grey-haired woman raised her hand. "I will come. It might be helpful and consoling if an elderly person is with you." She was plump and had a round, friendly face. If Armand was the epitome of a vampire, a tall, dark, brooding fellow, then Benedicta was just the opposite. She could have been anyone's aunt or mother.

"Thank you, Benedicta. You're very thoughtful and kind to come with us. I assure you, we won't fly too fast, so you can keep up with us," Joliette replied, smiling.

Joliette turned to face her coven again and said, "The three of us will leave tonight. Now, it's time to rest. We'll have a lot of work to do tonight. I hope you all understand that the new members of this coven will not be capable of finding nourishment by themselves, so they will follow you and learn. If you can, please help them to adjust to this new life. The faster they learn, the sooner they will proceed with their outside lives on their own."

Joliette yawned. "Good night, you all," she said, standing up, walking out of the meeting chamber, and heading to her resting room deeper in the catacombs. She had chosen it in the early days of the catacomb and decided to stay there. No human came that far in the catacombs nowadays, and thus, it was safe for her to sleep there. It was a small chamber with an opening on the wall. She had placed blankets there to make her rest more comfortable. She had not dragged any mattress or a bed down here. She knew this was only a temporary residence.

Chapter Five

Henri

Henri D'Ardent lay still in his cold cell in the Bastille.

He remembered the instructions of the beautiful woman who had given her the kiss of death. *Or perhaps it was a kiss of life,* Henri thought. He would live, but he would be like the living dead. He closed his eyes tight and pulled the blanket over his head. Soon,

Henri heard steps behind his cell door, and the keys clattered against the iron lock.

"Wake up, you noble bastard!" the guard yelled by the open door. He was a bear of a man and stank like old wine and sweat. "Time to meet your lady Guillotine. You have a date with her this morning," he added and belly-laughed at his own joke.

Henri did not move. He did not breathe. He hoped that the guard would go away thinking he was dead. No such luck. The guard approached his cot, and pulled off the blanket, and repeated, "Wake up!" He poked him on the ribs with the end of his musket. When Henri didn't move, the guard shook him by the shoulder. He watched Henri there for a while, then said to himself, "Another dead nobleman. They must die in fear of the lady Guillotine. We don't even have to lop off their heads. What cowards they are!"

The guard pulled the blanket over Henri's body, walked out, and headed to the next room. A young, beautiful woman lay there on the floor. Her skin was pale, and her lips rosy. She didn't move when the guard approached her. He kicked her in the back, but she remained still.

The guard shook his head. Such a beautiful young woman and dead as a doornail. "Merde, another dead body!" The guard cursed and then moved on. *Altogether, eight dead this morning,* he thought. *These aristocrats are weak and can't survive any changes in their rich lifestyle. Fear had made their hearts stop,* he thought, and went to report the deaths to his superior officer.

The gravediggers were ordered to pick up the dead bodies from their cells and carry them outside, where the bodies were dumped in a large body pile. From there, the corpses were later taken to Saint Marguerite Cemetery, which was one of the four cemeteries used to dispose of the corpses of the aristocrats killed in the guillotine during the French Revolution. The other cemeteries were bigger, whereas Saint Marguerite Cemetery was built in a common ditch. The revolutionists joked that the lords and ladies had lived in luxury and died in the hands of the Commoners and were buried in poverty in a trench.

Henri waited impatiently for his body to be picked up and carried out. When the gravediggers came, they double-checked the body making sure the guard had not made a mistake. One of them commented. "Don't let his fingers grab you. If he's still dying, his death grip will be so hard, that we'll have to break his fingers to unlock the grip."Henri laid still, making sure he did not breath or move a muscle before the grave diggers had checked his body.

"He's dead like a doornail," the other man confirmed before wrapping him in a burlap sack leaving the blanket in the cell for the next prisoner.

Next, they carried his body in between them through the corridors and threw it onto a pile of bodies. More bodies were added to the gruesome pile, weighing Henri down beneath their collective mass. Trapped beneath the mounting corpses, Henri's mind reeled, but he gripped onto reason. Deep breaths soothed his frantic heartbeat.

I'm beyond harm, he reassured himself. *The guards can't claim me twice.*

Next, Henri felt sharp teeth sinking into his leg and a sharp pain. A rat bit his leg! Henri kicked the rat, hoping that nobody was watching the bodies at that moment. The rat realized it had found a living person and crawled further away, thinking that there were plenty of bodies to eat. Henri sighed. He would still have to wait for sunset before he could leave this dump.

Chapter Six

The Undead

While waiting for the night, Henri recalled the weird night. He was sure he was going to be taken to the guillotine and then this strange woman arrived out of nowhere. She was more like a dream now in his mind.

Did it really happen, or was it just my imagination? Henri wondered, but then he knew something strange had happened during the night because his mind was working, he could move his limbs, and even if he was buried under the dead bodies, he could escape from his predicament when the sunset. He remembered the warning: stay out of the sunshine. He planned to obey the woman's orders to stay alive.

Henri wished the time would pass fast. He hated the stench of death around him. The rats squirmed inside the growing mountain of dead bodies, but when Henri moved, they went to the other bodies. He knew he couldn't move too much because that could alert the guards if they were outside or watching the pile. He doubted it, though, as they were not the sharpest and seemed tired of their duties carrying the dead bodies. Henri based his assumption on their behavior and words he had overheard when they carried out other bodies after his.

His thoughts were interrupted when another hand grabbed his hand. At first, Henri thought it was a guard who had noticed his subtle movements when he kicked the rats away, and he tried to stay very still. But the hand didn't pull his hand or let him go.

Perhaps it is a dead man's grip, Henri thought. He had heard that the hand of a deceased person could hold something so tight the undertakers had to wait for the grip to loosen for many hours if they didn't want to break the fingers. He didn't know why that happened.

Henri tried to pull his hand away slowly and carefully, but the hand gripped his even tighter and squeezed it. Henri realized he had a fellow undead buried next to him. He stopped struggling and let the person get comfort by holding his hand.

So, he and his new friend held hands for hours. They didn't know how late it was.

From time to time, Henri heard the guards coming by, throwing a new body into the pile and talking when they passed. Their shouts echoed from the courtyard.

Eventually, everything went quiet.

Now, it must be evening, Henri thought. He started moving his legs and then his shoulders and arms. His undead friend did the same, and together, they pushed away the bodies over them. There were only six, so they were lucky that they were not buried under dozens of them.

The rats ran over their legs, scared or surprised by their sudden movements. Henri shivered. He had always hated those creepy rodents.

He sat up and looked around. No guards anywhere. The cadaverous pile stank of rot and decay. Henri crouched and stood up. No shouts, no running footsteps, and no fired muskets. The guards had left the dead body pile for the night.

When Henri looked around, the sun had set. The sky was inky blue, and the stars were blinking.Then he remembered the other person. He glanced behind and saw a beautiful young woman sitting next to the dead bodies. He held out his hand and said, "I'm Henri."

"I'm Minette," the woman replied. Henri pulled her up next to him. He asked, "Did a woman visit you last night?"

"Yes, she promised me a life instead of the guillotine, and I accepted." The woman brushed her long hair behind her shoulders and turned her violet eyes to him. She was dirty and pale, but alive.

"I wasn't sure if I dreamed all of it," Henri admitted. "It felt so unreal today when I was i tossed away like garbage with the dead bodies."

"Yes, that was horrifying," the woman replied, shivering. "The rats bit me." She leaned down and looked at her leg, and she had a circle of bite marks there but no blood.

"They bit me too, but I think they noticed that we were not like the other bodies, so eventually, they left us alone," Henri replied.

"We didn't bleed, so they lost interest," Minette said, adding, "What do we do now?"

"The woman said someone will come by and escort us to safety. We'll have to wait for her help to show up." Henri looked around and said, "Let's descend and wait over there. I don't like this stench." He pointed out a place near the wall of the Bastille where they would be hidden from the plain view, but still, they could see the body mountain and if someone approached the pile. However, it did not take long before they had to run and crawl under the bodies again, because the gravediggers approached, and they knew they should not be seen near the bodies because the gravediggers would alert the guards, and they would be shot or imprisoned again - neither one of the choices was good.

Chapter Seven

The New Vampires Meet the Ancient Ones

Armand, Joliette, and Benedicta waited until the sun had set, then got ready to leave the catacombs. They flew out as bats and vanished into the dark night. No one would pay much attention to three flying bats at nighttime because they were black and almost invisible.

Joliette took the lead and headed to the infamous prison, the Bastille. She could see its heavy stone walls and ominous silhouette in the distance. *It's a landmark of desperation, pain, and misery,* she thought.

Joliette had lived for centuries, and thus she recalled the better days and could see what had led to this uprising. Several bad harvest years, drought, and cattle diseases had made the whole country starve, and the bread prices were so high that the peasants could not afford to get any. Also, the king and the regime raised taxes and took even the little the common people had left of their money, which wasn't much. Thus, looting and rioting were normal in the cities. Even now, late at night, the people were attacking the carriages on the narrow cobblestone streets and robbing them, leaving the passengers hurt or dead. Violence on the streets was not uncommon. The insurgency culminated in the event of July 14th when the rioters attacked the Bastille, trying to get more gunpowder and weapons. That happened over six months ago. The uprising was still ongoing, and the aristocratic families were in danger in any city.

When the bats reached the prison, they circled to see that guards were not paying attention to the pile of dead bodies before they landed next to it. Transforming back to their human forms, the vampires walked around the pile, trying to find the new vampires.

Joliette had told them to be still until dark, and she hoped they had obeyed her; otherwise, they would not have survived in the sunshine.

"Hello?" Joliette called out. Her eyes scanned the large body pile. A slight movement on the pile made her turn, and she saw rats running away. Then, an arm appeared. Someone was there. She gestured to the others to come and help, and they quickly moved the dead bodies that covered the new vampires. Henri and Minette climbed out. Both looked almost intact if you don't consider a few rat bite marks and dirty, stained clothes.

"We had to hide again, because the gravediggers came by," Henri explained. "I didn't see anyone else alive beside us."

She gestured for them to keep their voices down and kept looking. She had saved more than two. *Where are the others?* When Armand and Benedicta followed her, she whispered, "Six more."

"We have to move the bodies from the top. They could be buried so deep they can't get out," Armand suggested.

With their supernatural strength, it was easy to move the bodies, and soon, they found two other women. They were scared but alive. "I'm Claudine," one of them said and the other woman added, "I'm Rosette." They were both young ladies from upper-class families separated from their family members.

Benedicta helped them climb down the pile of dead bodies and then returned up to help with the digging. They moved the bodies until Joliette gestured to stop.

"These are older bodies. See how they are decomposing. The others I saved are not here."

They descended the pile, and Armand said, "What if their sentencing is postponed?"

Joliette glanced at him and said, "If that happened, then they are dead. They couldn't have avoided the sunshine if they were taken to the court in bright daylight."

"They could also be still in their cells," Benedicta replied.

"I'll go and check it out. Better be sure we didn't leave anyone behind. You two take care of the four new vampires. They will need blood, and then you should all go back to the catacombs," Joliette commanded.

With a graceful twirl, Adele's form shifted, her body dissolving into the sleek, dark shape of a bat. She soared upward, her leathery wings beating effortlessly as she followed the castle wall, pausing to peer into the narrow windows of the cells.

Most of the cells were empty, waiting for new oc-
cupants. So, that meant the others were taken away
during the daytime. She flew back across the velvety
night sky. She only stopped to have some nutrition
herself: a deserted alley and a young man walking
alone was a perfect victim. She didn't waste any time,
and soon, she was back in the air as a bat heading to
the catacombs.

Chapter Eight

The First Drink of Blood

Meanwhile, Armand and Benedicta led the new vampires through the quiet night streets of Paris. Their steps echoed on the cobblestones as they proceeded cautiously toward the catacombs. They didn't want to be seen by the patrols, who still walked around the streets looking for aristocrats. As they heard a couple of guards approaching, they withdrew to a doorway and waited until the men had passed before continuing to their destination.

Both Armand and Minette stunk and looked horrible: bloody-stained and ripped clothes and the rotten smell from the body pile. Rosette and Claudine did not look any better.

Henri had never walked in a nighttime Paris before. He'd always rode a horse or sat in a carriage. He took a deep breath. The air smelled like urine in the narrow alleys because the citizens peed outside wherever they got the urge. As they walked further on, the delicious aroma of cooked onion reached his nose. He realized that his senses were sharper than before and that he could hear and smell better.

Grey and black rats crossed their paths. Henri even considered grabbing one as he was getting hungry. He had not eaten for two days, he counted.

"Can we stop and eat?" he whispered to their guides.

Benedicta cackled. "Sure, but remember you're not a human any longer. You'll want different nourishment than before." With these words, she gestured to a drunken man ahead of them. "That should do for a snack now." She walked ahead and grabbed the man by the arm, and then quickly, before the man could react, she bit him on the neck and gestured for Armand and Minette to come and share her prey.

Armand stood guarding them while they used the drunken man as their nourishment.

When Henri saw the bloody neck, he felt a strange urge inside of him. He had never felt anything so strong. It was a primordial craving. He crouched next to the victim and placed his mouth on his bleeding neck. Henri didn't know how to suck the blood, so he bit his neck and then tried to drink it. "No, you need to suck it," Benedicta corrected him.

After Henri had got some blood in him, Benedicta pulled him away and said, "Leave something for the ladies too." He shared the body with Claudine and Rosette. Armand shook his head, "You need some practice."

Next was Minette turn. She leaned closer and opened her beautiful mouth, her canines shining in the moonlight. She sank her teeth into the soft skin of the neck and sucked hard.

"You're a natural vampire!" Benedicta praised Minette as she stood up, wiping the extra blood off her plump lips. She glanced at Henri and, shaking her head, added, "And you, not so much... You need to practice drinking your blood quickly and efficiently."

Minette beamed. She felt strong after drinking the blood. "Thank you." She curtsied to Benedicta in the alley.

"Come on. We need to go. We have a long way to walk." Armand gestured for them to follow him. Quietly, they moved along the dark alleys, keeping an eye on anyone who could threaten them.

Minette whispered, "Why can't we transform into bats and fly like Joliette?"

"It will take some practice to learn to transform from a human body to a bat and then learn to fly. It doesn't happen with a snap of the fingers," Armand replied while surveying the houses and the streets ahead. "I can't teach you that now. Some of us vampires figure it out immediately, but some might need more time. However, we still have about an hour's walk left, so I wouldn't start showing you any new vampire tricks while we're still in danger," he advised, walking ahead with long strides and disappearing behind the next corner. "Keep close to me, so we don't get separated."

Chapter Nine

The Night Patrol

The moon cast eerie shadows on the narrow alleyway as Armand, Benedicta, Henri, and Minette huddled together, their whispers urgent.

"Be careful and silent! The night patrol is increasing its rounds." Armand warned, glancing over his shoulder. "They have started using silver bullets in fear of us. They know we exist in the city's underbelly, but they don't know where our coven is."

Benedicta nodded, her eyes scanning the dark street ahead of them. "We can't risk being caught."

Just then, the sound of boots echoed through the side alley, growing louder. Minette's grip on Henri's arm tightened. Rosette inhaled quickly and grabbed Claudine's arm.

"That must be them," Henri whispered, his eyes locked onto the approaching patrol.

The night patrol, their faces obscured by tricornes and scarves, marched into view. Torches cast flickering shadows on the walls as they fanned out, surrounding the group.

"Arrêtez!" one of the patrolmen barked. "You are under arrest for suspected counter-revolutionary activities."

Armand swiftly pushed Benedicta and Minette ahead. "Go!"

Henri's gaze went from them to the other vampires trying to decide what to do.

"Come on, Henri!" Armand urged.

But it was too late. The patrolmen closed in on him too; their muskets trained on Henri. "You, stay where you are." The leader hit him on the head with the butt of his musket as he tried to run away.

Armand, Benedicta, and Minette slipped into the shadows by a nearby building's doorway, disappearing from the patrol's view.

The night patrol's torches cast flickering shadows on the alleyway walls, illuminating Claudine and Rosette's terrified faces. The two women cowered, their hands quickly bound behind their backs. They were too scared to use their new vampire skills to fight back.

Armand and Benedicta emerged from the darkness, their eyes glowing like embers in the night. Their faces elongated, fangs bared, and skin pale as alabaster.

The patrolmen froze, paralyzed by fear, as the two vampires descended upon them.

Armand's fangs sank into the patrol leader's neck, his eyes flashing with supernatural fury. Benedicta's nails shredded the uniforms of the other patrolmen, her movements a blur.

The alleyway erupted into chaos. The patrolmen's screams mingled with the sound of ripping fabric and snapping bones. Claudine and Rosette stumbled backward, horror-stricken.

"Henri!" Armand called out, his voice low, as he discarded the patrol leader's lifeless body.

But Henri didn't respond. He lay motionless, struck by a patrolman's musket butt.

Benedicta's gaze locked onto Henri's still form. "We must leave him," she whispered, her voice barely audible over the patrolmen's dying screams.

Armand's face contorted in anguish, but he knew Benedicta was right. They couldn't risk exposure.

With a snarl, Armand pulled Claudine and Rosette with them, and they vanished into the night, leaving Henri behind. Minette had watched the event unfolding from the doorway and as the others came by, she said, "We can't leave Henri behind."

"What can we do?" Armand responded. "My task was to bring you to our coven. I can't risk being late. You will die at sunrise if you are outside."

Minette stared at him, knowing he was right. There was nothing to do to save Henri.

Armand's grip tightened around Claudine's hand and Rosette followed as he sprinted through the winding alleys, Benedicta and Minette followed close by. The night air was heavy with the scent of urine and smoke.

"We're almost to the coven's sanctuary," Armand whispered, his fangs retracted, his eyes scanning the road ahead.

But fate had other plans.

A silver-tipped bullet whizzed past Armand's ear, striking Claudine with a sickening thud. She crumpled in his arms, her eyes wide with shock, her immortal life force ebbing away.

"Non! Claudine!" Rosette screamed, clinging to her.

Benedicta spun around, her eyes blazing with fury, as the patrol emerged from the shadows.

Armand tried to shield the women, but it was too late. Another silver-tipped bullet struck Rosette, and she slumped against him, her body limp.

Benedicta attacked the night patrol, killing them in a flash. Armand went to assist and then returned to the two bodies.

"Claudine... Rosette..." Armand whispered, his voice cracking with anguish.

Benedicta's face twisted in a snarl. "We must leave them. We can't risk exposure."

Armand hesitated, his heart heavy with grief. He gently laid Claudine and Rosette on the cobblestones, his eyes fixed on their lifeless forms. Their bodies will vanish in the first sunlight, he knew that. "Mon Dieu," he whispered, his voice barely audible. "Their immortal lives lost."

Benedicta's grip on his arm tightened. "We cannot stay. The hunters will return."

With a heavy heart, Armand followed Benedicta and Minette into the night, leaving behind the two vampires they had sworn to protect.

Their ashes would scatter in the wind. Henri, still unconscious, would never know the fate of his fellow vampires.

The darkness closed in around the escaping vampires, their footsteps echoing through the deserted alleys.

"We should have tried to save Henri," Armand whispered, his eyes staring in the dark.

Benedicta's voice was barely audible. "We tried to save all of them. We failed."

Their silence was a heavy shroud, weighing them down as they vanished into the underbelly of the city where the buried bodies lay in rest in catacombs.

Chapter Ten

Joliette

J oliette paced in the catacombs, waiting for Armand, Benedicta, and the new vampires to return. *They should have been back by now,* she thought. She went to the entrance and looked around. No sign of them. Nobody was out this time. The night was almost over. She could see the narrow line of the sunrise lighting the early morning sky on the horizon.

She turned to go back inside the catacombs when she heard running footsteps approaching. Turning around, she surveyed the area ahead of her. And there they were: Armand, Benedicta, and—only one fledgling vampire! What had happened?

She tapped her feet and waited for the vampires to approach, and hastily, they all went inside the darkness of the catacombs. Joliette led the small group inside to the larger cave, where more vampires stayed and rested.

She stopped and faced the three vampires. "What happened?" Her eyes flashed with worry.

"The night patrol!" Armand looked apologetic.

"Explain!" Joliette wanted an explanation, staring angrily at her two trusted vampires.

Benedicta replied, "The night patrol came by, and we had to flee. We could have fought them off, but then the young man was hit on his head. We couldn't carry him away. We left him there in the alley with the night patrol and fled."

"And the others?" Joliette asked.

"They were shot with silver bullets, and dead immediately," Armand replied looking sad.

Joliette cursed. She'd done so much to grow her coven, but now she only had one new vampire. All the others were lost, either dead or captured.

She took a deep breath and glanced at the young woman who had survived. "Welcome to my coven. We met before. Tell me your name again."

"Minette, ma'am," the new vampire replied, curtsying.

"No need to do any of that. We call ourselves by our first names. That's easiest." Joliette replied and added, "Find yourself a place to rest. It will be dawn soon. We vampires rest when the sun rises and go out to feed when it sets."

"Thank you, Joliette, for saving me and bringing me here." Minette looked grateful.

"We'll get you new clothes tomorrow," Joliette said. "You can wash in a river when the sun sets," she added.

Minette nodded and looked around curiously as she walked away with Benedicta. The bones and the skulls on the wall caves interested her. She stopped and touched some bones. "This is a burial chamber, isn't it?"

"Yes, it is," Benedicta confirmed. "More bodies are buried here than above the ground." She pointed at smaller caves and said, "Sleep in any of those rooms. We'll wake you up when it's time to go out and hunt."

"Thank you," Minette replied, choosing the first cave. She lay on the stone and gravel ground of the cave.

"You can find some blankets tomorrow to make your rest more comfortable," Benedicta added. "Have a good sleep."

Minette closed her eyes. Her new life had begun, but its start had not been easy. Her new friend, Henri, was lost to the night guards, and she barely escaped herself. Sighing, she turned to her other side, trying to fall asleep, but the sleep didn't come because of all the action that had happened earlier. She played the scene over and over again in her head, trying to figure out if she or the others could have done anything to save Henri. Finally, she fell into a restless sleep.

Chapter Eleven

What Happened to Henri?

Back at the alley where the Night Patrol attacked the vampires

"This man is not alive. He's not breathing," one of the patrol men told to his captain.

"He must have died when he hit the cobblestones. Leave him there. We don't carry any bodies during our patrol," the captain of the Night Patrol replied. "Let's move on."

As the patrol walked away, they had no idea that Henri was just unconscious.

After fifteen minutes went by, Henri stirred, blinking his eyes. He did not remember what had happened. He saw the carnage with dead night patrol around him and realized Armand and the others must have killed them.

Where am I? he wondered, and then he recalled the walk from the Bastille with the other vampires and the patrol. He sat up and touched the back of his head with his hand.

I'm going to have a huge egg-size bump at the back of my head, Henri thought, wincing. *Whoever hit me from behind whacked my head hard – again!* He stood up, but he felt a bit dizzy. He leaned on the stone wall and took deep breaths, trying to get his world to stay still.

Looking around, Henri tried to find the others, but they were long gone by now.

They must be alive. They are heading to the catacombs; I know that much, Henri thought. *Can I find my way there by myself? I must try. I won't survive alone because I don't know anything about being a vampire in this city. I don't even know this city so well. I don't have any money with me, and I look and stink like a beggar.*

He started walking toward the end of the alley where they had been heading when the patrol had surprised their journey.

He glanced up to the sky. The horizon was getting brighter, he noticed nervously. *I have to find a place to stay during the daytime. I can't stay out in daylight, or I will die,* he worried.

Running, he passed several alleys and then came to a cemetery area. *Can I find a way into the catacombs here?* He looked around and saw a church and then the Saints-Innocents cemetery.

Two quarry workers were starting their day early, or so Henri thought. What he did not know was that they had worked all night, and this was their last load of skeletons from the graves and charnel houses in this area tonight.

The other worker said, "This is the last one. Let's take the bones from that grave and then head to the catacombs. We don't want the citizens or the priests to see us digging up graves. They would behead us." And they were right about that. The city wanted the cemeteries and the bodies to be transported outside the city limits for health reasons. The workers had to do their gruesome tasks at nighttime when no one observed their work.

Henri sighed in relief. This would save him, and he'd find his way to the other vampires.

Henri paced impatiently as he saw them digging up graves and piling skeletons into their cart. When the workers looked away, he snuck to the cart, climbed in, and buried himself under the skeletons and bones. The quarry workers had a full cart soon, and they climbed on the driver's seat and headed outside Paris to the catacombs, where they would dump all the bones into galleries within.

Henri rode on the cart with them, keeping his body covered under the bodies and bones so that the first sunrays would not bun and kill him.

When the quarry workers finally reached their destination, the sun was up on the horizon, bright orange and red.

They pushed the cart by the catacombs' entrance and emptied the load there on the first empty gallery. "Let's go to sleep. We have more work tonight," the other man said, and they both walked out.

Henri waited a while until he couldn't hear their steps any longer, and then he climbed out of the bone pile. He was still alive. Now, he had to find the others.

Chapter Twelve

How to Survive

Joliette was disappointed as she had lost the new vampires. Only Minette was now transformed into a vampire. She had spent all night transforming the prisoners, but now it seemed a waste of time. If only one would be saved, was it even worth trying?

She closed her eyes to rest, but no sleep came. She kept listening to the smallest sounds in the catacombs:

the mice scurrying across the floor, the bats flying and screeching, and the footsteps...

Footsteps?

She opened her eyes, quickly got up, and headed toward the sound of the steps. Who could be walking around inside the catacomb this time? It was still night. Usually, the night workers stayed outside. They only dumped the bodies in large piles and then left the quarry. Besides, those workers stank to a high heaven of sweat, dirt, and meat, but this one. This man had a different scent. She could smell the dirt, mold, and decay on him, but not the meaty scent like normal humans. Her heart leaped. What if—

Could it even be possible—

To move faster, she transformed into a bat and flew fast through the winding corridors and gravesites until she saw the man. Landing in front of him in the dark aisle, she changed back to the woman Henri had seen in the prison.

It was him! The one she had saved inside the Bastille. The one who was supposed to arrive with Minette but was lost on the way here. How did he find this place? How could he be alive? She had so many questions as she approached the dirty and tired-looking young aristocrat.

"Henri," she greeted him, smiling and revealing her beautiful white teeth. She raised her arms to embrace him. "Come here." She grabbed him in her arms, and he shivered. She felt his knees buckling. He needed nourishment and fast. The stress always burned the energy fast and required replenishment, new blood.

"Have you eaten anything lately?" She stared at his face.

"Yes, when I was with the others," Henri said. "We stopped one young drunken man and drank his blood."

"That's not enough for you. You had to fight your way out of there, I guess, and somehow you managed to get here. What little you drank was not sufficient for all that physical activity. I'll take you out to find some blood now," Joliette replied. "Come with me."

Henri followed Joliette through the winding paths inside the catacomb to a gate. They stepped outside. It was still night for a couple of hours, but they had to hurry. They couldn't go too far because they needed to return underground before sunrise.

Joliette led him to a square nearby, then turned to the next side alley and again to the right. She didn't want to run because she wasn't sure how strong Henri was. She didn't want him to pass out before they found a suitable body.

After the next corner, she spotted a body. A beggar was in front of them, sleeping in the alley. Joliette snuck up on him, bit him on the neck to subdue him, and next, she waved Henri to come closer. "Now, drink. We have to return soon."

Henri crouched next to the man and drank his blood – all of it. Joliette watched him pleased. The young man acted like a real vampire. She was proud of him. Proud because he had survived alone, proud because he didn't panic when he was left alone, and proud also because he had good vampire instincts, which not many new vampires had.

When Henri finished, he wiped his bloody mouth with the back of his hand, stood up, and stared at his victim. His eyes were glassy and his teeth red. "What will happen to him?" He felt the rush of the new blood inside him, and energy swelled in his body. He wasn't so exhausted as before.

"He will die." Joliette's voice was cold. "No one survives losing that much blood. However, it was his life or yours, and I chose you over him. He was a beggar and had no life. You had a life that was cruelly taken away for political reasons, and you were thrown to prison for no reason at all. You deserved a second chance."

Henri searched for his own feelings. Was he sorry? Yes, he didn't want to kill anyone. He veered his eyes on Joliette and said, "I understand. It's a fight for survival. I can only survive if I take someone else's blood. I will continue doing that because I don't want to die."

Joliette beamed. He was a good choice for a vampire. He knew what it meant to be one. A game of survival. Yes, that's what this life was. She nodded. "Yes, you're correct." She glanced at the sky. It was turning paler. The night would soon be over. "We need to hurry back to the catacombs." She grabbed his hand and pulled him with her. They ran the same way they had walked and went through the gate before the first sun rays hit the ground.

Joliette led him through the catacombs and showed him where the others were. All of them were asleep. They didn't bother to wake up when they heard Joliette's whisper. She wasn't a danger. Her voice brought them solace.

Chapter Thirteen

Where to Go Next?

From the dawn of time the vampires had existed; moving silently down through the centuries, living many secret lives, struggling to find a new role and place to live. The mortal humans rarely knew the vampires were among them ... until they met one and either died or became one.

Joliette stared at the skulls filling the caves in the catacombs. She did not know any of them, but she was sure some of her lineage would be somewhere there. She felt so old. As a human she would have been dead a long time ago – too long to even count the years. She had seen different styles of clothes, wars, famine, and kings and queens ascend to their throne and die.

Maybe it was time for a new start.

She had finally decided to leave Paris and head for the new continent, the Americas. She had heard so much about it. She had secretly listened to Benjamin Franklin when he visited France in 1776. That was before this craziness of Madame Guillotine and killing all the aristocrats happened. She had enough money and jewels to buy that luxury for herself. She could start anew there.

Benjamin Franklin had visited the king in Versailles, and while they had walked outside in the lavish garden and admired the fountains and the statues, Joliette dressed as one of the aristocrats and pretended to be one of the queen's ladies-in-waiting. Eagerly, she had listened to everything he had told King Louis XVI about the new continent. After that evening, she was sure the new country was her destiny and destination. She had enough money to travel there and take her coven with her. They could settle somewhere in the south where it would be warm and buy several mansions. She would rather live in a real building than in a catacomb. She knew most of her coven would follow her as she was their creator. However, she was not sure about the new members. They should be given the choice to stay in France or follow the others.

Meanwhile, Henri was so tired that he collapsed in the nearest cavern, which was empty. He knew he stank to the high heaven, but he had no change of clothes or even water to clean himself. Longingly, he recalled his family estate and wondered if the peasants had taken it. The commoners had come for him, but he didn't know what happened to his fortune. His mansion was most likely emptied and robbed clean, and all the valuables, including money and jewelry, had been stolen, he guessed. He also knew he had a secret room, which he was sure the Commoners could not have found. All the old castles had secret passages and rooms in them, and his home was no different. If he could get there, he could get clean clothes, money, and perhaps even stay there. Or could he stay there? The commoners would come after him again, wouldn't they? He hoped some of his servants had stayed, and perhaps, they would still be loyal to him. The more he thought about it, the more he wanted to go and see what condition his home was in. He could then decide what to do. When he finally fell asleep, he slept like a rock. He didn't move or snore. He laid still as the dead.

Chapter Fourteen

Joliette

The next evening, Joliette gathered all the vampires around her and said, "I have decided to leave for the new continent. I will give you all the option to stay or come with me. Even if I'm your creator and you belong to my coven now, I don't want to force anyone to leave their home. It has to be voluntary. We, vampires, live forever, and I would not want any one of you to suffer living in a place where you don't want to be." She looked around and saw nods, but also some wary looks. "I have bought us a pass on a tall ship to take us there. We must divide to stay in two parts of the ship: berth and orlop. Five of us will stay in the berth, which is the living and sleeping quarters, and rest will stay in the orlop usually used as storage. There should be plenty of room for all of us, but because it will take us a long time to sail to our destination, we have to undergo hibernation to conserve human blood within our bodies during the journey when sufficient vital fluid is scarce."

She looked around and saw puzzled gazes. She realized that some of the vampires didn't even know what hibernation was. "A hibernation phase is something we vampires use when we can't get enough human blood, and thus, we go to a state of deep sleep and are programmed to wake up when the nutrition is available."

Some whispers and murmurs, but no clear acceptance or denial, she thought. That was good. They would have time to decide. "I will wake up first when we reach our destination because I'm the queen of this coven. I will then wake up the rest of you, so you don't have to worry about that."

Henri took a few steps forward and said, "Miss Joliette, I would like to join you later. I want to go to my castle first and see if anything salvageable is left there. I want to see my home one more time before I leave France."

"That's not a good idea," Joliette said, shaking her head. "The commoners are looking for all the escaped aristocrats and will find you. You can't trust anyone. You can't reveal that you are a vampire. How do you think you can survive alone?"

"I will find a way to get there alive," Henri said, determined.

Joliette's eyes latched on his, and she considered this young man and his qualities. "You survived when everyone else believed you would die. You managed to find our coven, even if you were not Parisian and didn't know where the catacombs were." She nodded. "I think if anyone can do what you said, you can. I will leave you the address where I'm going, and you can come after us if you wish. Send me a word when you come, and I will come to the harbor to wake you up."

Henri bowed, smiling. "Thank you, milady. I will find you. I promise."

The meeting took another hour, and afterward, the vampires went hunting in the night streets of Paris. It wasn't difficult to find beggars or drunkards.

Chapter Fifteen

Henri Travels Back Home

Upon waking the following evening, Henri discovered a heap of clothing strewn about his cavern. Hastily, he swapped his attire for cleaner garments, leaving the soiled ones behind. Venturing forth, he sought out his companions, finding them congregating alongside Joliette at the cavern's entrance.

Joliette's eyes met Henri's. "We're prepared to depart from this city. What are your plans?" Joliette inquired.

"I shall return to my home," Henri responded. "I'll join you later when I have settled my affairs, but I require your assistance."

"Pray tell, what do you need?" Joliette asked, intrigued.

"Teach me the art of transforming into a bat."

Joliette's laughter reverberated throughout the cave. "It's simple. You must focus on the change, beginning with your hands, and envision yourself as a bat."

Henri's eyes shone with pride as he settled back into his human form, his transformation into a bat now effortless.

"Well done, Henri," Joliette praised, her smile warm. "Now, let's discuss the finer points of vampiric etiquette."

Henri leaned in, eager to learn. "I want to know everything."

"Drinking blood, for instance," Joliette began. "A couple of minutes should suffice for quick nourishment. Ten minutes will sustain you for a day. But beware, Henri: drain the human completely, and they'll perish. Leave a mere pinch of blood, and... well, you'll create a new vampire – a fledgling like you."

Henri's eyebrows shot up. "A fledgling?"

Joliette nodded, her eyes sparkling. "Yes, that's what they are called. And their creators, like myself, are called sires or, in my case, milady."

"And what happens to the human if I don't kill them?" Henri asked, curiosity getting the better of him.

Joliette's gaze turned serious. "They'll awaken later, likely with a headache and nausea. Younger victims tend to recover better; older ones may succumb to stress."

Henri nodded thoughtfully.

"When you're ready to join me in the New World," Joliette continued, "ensure you have a secure coffin for travel. No one must open it during daylight."

Henri's expression turned grim. "Or I'll perish."

Joliette's concern was palpable. "You're still learning to hibernate, Henri. You'll likely wake up each night. Find fresh blood to sustain yourself, and protect yourself during the day. The voyage will be treacherous."

Henri's determination faltered, but he squared his shoulders. "I'll manage."

Joliette's eyes narrowed. "I worry about you traveling alone. It's safer with our coven."

Henri's heart ached, knowing he couldn't leave yet. "I'll find a way," he repeated, trying to sound resolute.

Joliette's gaze lingered on him, as if searching for assurance. "Very well, Henri. Promise me you'll join us soon."

"I promise," Henri replied, his mind racing with the challenges ahead.

The vampires left the catacombs that night.

Joliette hugged Henri and French-kissed him on both cheeks before she held him at arms-length and said, "Henri, take care of yourself. You will always have a home in my coven. Come and find me when you've done what you think you still need to do here." She handed him a folded piece of paper. "The name of the ship we'll depart on, and the destination is Boston Harbor. I don't yet know the exact location where we will stay. I will try to leave you a note at the harbor with the harbor master or in a tavern if possible."

Henri never dreamt of traveling that far, but now that he had an eternity to spend, he could do it. "I will come and find you." He waved at the group as they walked together towards the harbor, and Henri left them and headed out of Paris to his family estate. He used his new gift of transforming into a bat and flew over the city walls. *Everything looks so small down there*, he thought. He recalled the warning Joliette had said, "Remember to keep enough fluid in you. Otherwise, you will be too weak to feed yourself."

He flew for an hour, and when he saw some drunk-ards coming out of an inn, he circled above them. *One of them would be enough for me for the rest of the trip,* he thought. He waited as the other man went to the side of the building to relieve himself. Henri landed softly behind him and transformed back into a human, grabbed the man by the shoulder, and pulled his head and neck toward him. He sank his teeth in his neck and drank the life-giving red blood from his veins. He didn't take so much so that the man would not turn into a vampire, just enough that he would be able to travel forward. He was not yet sure how much that was, but he only drank for two minutes hoping that it would be enough for him to survive the next part of his trip.

When he was satisfied, he lowered the man in the alley, transformed back into a bat, and flew up toward the starry sky.

That man's friends will find him there and think he was just too drunk to stay awake, Henri thought.

It was faster to travel by flying than with a carriage. He was able to cross areas that the carriage and horses could not go through, and thus, the distance between Paris and his hometown was shorter than he had estimated. In two hours, he saw the familiar village ahead, and his estate loomed behind it on a hill. He flapped his wings faster, and soon, he was at the gates and flew over them. *Home,* he thought as he flew past the oak-tree-lined road that led to the front of the mansion.

Circling the building, he made sure no one was there. He didn't see any servants, villagers, or commoners nearby.

He landed by the last trees, transformed into his human body, and walked toward the front door. It was ajar.

Furrowing his brows, he stepped inside and saw the chaos. His ancestors' portraits were torn or thrown on the wall, and the drawers of the dressers and tables were opened and emptied on the floor. As he walked past, he saw that some windows were broken. Most of the valuable silverware was taken, as were the copper pots from the kitchen.

He wanted to cry and yell at someone. Why did this happen to him? He and his family had never done anything wrong to the villagers. He had always treated his servants well.

He went upstairs to his bedroom and saw that most of his clothes had been taken, but he found some old pants and shirts left behind. His parents' bedroom was also tossed. He returned to the library and his study, where a secret safe was hidden behind his father's portrait. He hoped that it would be intact. The safe was such an interesting invention for wealthy people that he didn't believe any commoner would know what it was even if they had seen it. Just thirty years ago, his father heard about the invention of a steel-walled box to hide your valuables, and he immediately ordered one and installed it in the library room.

Henri saw that his father's portrait was still hanging on the wall. He went to it and turned it aside as it had hinges on the other side of the frame. The safe was there intact. He sighed in relief. Quickly, he opened it. All his gold coins, his parents' jewelry, cash, and other valuable papers like the ownership of this estate and his family tree and proof of their aristocracy were there.

I need a bag, he realized. He looked around and spotted an old satchel lying on the floor. He picked it up and stuffed it with the contents of the safe. He closed the safe's door again and turned the portrait back so that no one would know he had visited there.

I have money now to buy a house in the new country, Henri thought. He decided to check on the secret passages and rooms of the mansion. He recalled he and his parents had left some clothes and shoes there. The entrance was hidden behind the library room's fireplace. Henri pushed down one of the fireplace tiles, and a door opened at the back.

He stepped inside and saw no one had been there since he left. He didn't need the torch as he could see well in the dark. He followed the narrow path to a secret room and saw a cot, table, and chairs. And clothes hanging in a closet.

Good. I can stay overnight here and then leave tomorrow night. However, I need to stock up on more blood before the night is over. Quickly, he changed clothes and put on boots. He felt better wearing his own clothes. *Time to go*, he thought and returned the same way to the library and closed the secret entrance.

Walking back to the kitchen, he glanced outside. It was still dark. He left through the kitchen door as a bat again. He didn't want any villagers to see him as he didn't know whom he could trust and who would betray him to the commoners.

He flew to the nearest town and looked for an inn again, as they might have late visitors or drunken guests that could be easy to grab and use. He saw an elderly woman coming out of a house, but he decided to leave her alone. She didn't have that many years to live, and she would need all her blood, so he continued to fly over the town. Finally, he saw a young woman in her twenties. She came out of another building and looked like she was heading to the inn.

She's perfect. Her young body will recover fast, Henri decided, and watched her for a while, making sure no one was coming after her.

Henri transformed into a human behind her and said, "Good evening, my lady."

The young woman turned around, surprised, and when he saw a strapping young aristocrat, she sighed. "Oh, you scared me, milord."

"I didn't mean to. I was passing by, and my carriage broke its wheel. Could you show me a way to an inn?"

"Yes, of course," the young maid said, adding, "I was going there myself."

"How convenient." Henri smiled. "Show me the way."

As they walked past a dark alley, he pulled her with him before she had time to react or call for help. Sinking his sharp teeth in her soft neck skin, Henri drank her sweet blood with lust. When he had taken what he needed, he lifted his head and wiped his mouth.

"Don't worry, my dear girl. You'll be just fine. You won't turn into a night creature like me. You will wake up later, and you'll be nauseous, and your neck will hurt, but that's all."

When he heard approaching voices, he transformed into a bat and flew up in the air. Two men were talking as they came toward the same alley he had just left.

Henri knew they would soon find the girl, so he flew back to his estate and directly inside through the open front door. He made sure no one saw him, and he entered the secret room through the library again and closed the door behind him. He was tired but satisfied. Collapsing on the cot in the secret room, he closed his eyes. *Time to sleep.*

Chapter Sixteen

Henri's Young Victim

The villagers surrounded unconscious Adele, their faces twisted in fear and revulsion. "A demon's mark!" someone shouted. "She's been claimed by darkness!"

"A demon has gotten her! She should be burned!" The cry echoed through the crowd, fueled by superstition and terror.

Adele's father, Pierre, emerged from the inn, his eyes wide with horror. "No, no! Not my Adele!" He stumbled backward as if recoiling from a poisonous serpent.

The villagers began to argue, their voices rising. "Should we burn her?"

An elderly man, Jacques, pushed through the crowd, his eyes locked on Adele's swollen, blood-stained neck. "No burning. Banishment is enough."

The villagers murmured, some nodding in agreement. Jacques continued, "Carry her outside the village. Let her find her own path from there."

He spotted a sturdy cart and two able-bodied men, Gaston and Louis. "Take her," Jacques ordered, his voice firm. "Leave her beyond the village gates. When she awakens, keep your distance. Warn her off with pitchforks. Tell her never to return."

Gaston and Louis hesitated, but Jacques's authority swayed them. They carefully lifted Adele into the cart, her limp form swaying as they began their somber procession.

As they departed the village, the crowd watched, their faces etched with fear and suspicion. Pierre remained behind, his eyes fixed on the ground, his heart heavy with grief and shame.

The cart rattled beyond the village gates, Gaston and Louis exchanging uneasy glances. They halted, waiting for Adele to stir, their pitchforks at the ready.

After she finally woke up, they shouted at her, "Demon spawn! Leave this village alone. Go away!"

She looked puzzled as she didn't know what had happened.

Her neck ached.

"Why... what have I done to you?"

"You're a demon now. Your neck bears the marks of a night demon!"

She touched her neck, and when she looked at her fingers, she had a bit of dried blood on her fingertips. "But I didn't do anything."

The young woman stood up, brushed off her clothes, and tried to approach the two men.

"Get away from here!" the two men yelled angrily at the lone woman, brandishing their pitchforks as they ushered her to retreat even further.

As the woman stood there, the gravity of the situation washed over her. It was evident that these men were deadly serious. Panic surged within her, prompting her to gather the hem of her dress and flee in haste. At first, she had no clear destination in mind, so she gradually slowed her pace and eventually came to a stop, attempting to make sense of what was going on.

She covered her face with her hands. What had transpired? Her last recollection was strolling through the village the night before when a seemingly affable gentleman had approached her with a query. After that encounter, her memory drew a blank. It suddenly struck her that the aristocratic-looking man from the previous night was somehow responsible for her predicament. The realization crystallized as she remembered the portraits adorning the walls of the nearby castle, bearing an uncanny resemblance to him. She used to work there as a maid for a short while before The Jacobins had taken the heir away. *That's where I must go*, she thought. If this man was the count's relative or the count himself, then he was responsible for her banishment, and he held the key to her salvation.

She embarked on a daunting nighttime trek toward the impressive estate. The eerie nocturnal sounds in the darkness caused her to startle at every rustle, the unsettling shadows quickening her heart rate. Nevertheless, she did not turn back. She could not.

As she reached the oak-tree-lined road, a path that wound its way toward the grand estate's front, she paused and stared at the building hoping that she was right about the man who did this to her.

A sigh of relief escaped her lips when she observed that the entrance door was slightly ajar. It was an encouraging sign, offering a sliver of hope amidst the uncertainty that had brought her here. She snuck inside. The hinges barely creaked as she gingerly pulled the door closed behind her, enveloping herself in the dimly lit interior. Cautiously, she ventured further into the hall, her footsteps echoing on the polished floors. Room after room revealed no signs of life. She saw broken chairs, plates, and torn fabrics, telling her that the place had been looted after she had been here the last time.

Undeterred, she ascended a grand staircase, her gaze drawn to the portraits thrown on the floor and some still adorning the walls. As her eyes fell upon those painted visages, a flood of memories rushed back to her. She had been here in this very place before, albeit briefly, during a period of time before the revolution had swept through the land. She recalled how she was shown the great hall and the staircase when she first took her position as a maid. She started working in the kitchen, and sometimes she took the tray upstairs to Countess D'Ardent.

The young woman eventually stumbled upon a spacious bedroom. The room offered comfort amidst the foreboding that enveloped the estate. It was here, amid the fading grandeur of the aristocratic family, that she decided to spend the night, opting to defer her decisions until the following day.

With a heavy sigh, she lowered herself onto the bed, the soft sheets offering a semblance of respite. Exhaustion washed over her, and soon, she succumbed to sleep's gentle embrace. However, nightmares unfurled like ominous specters, casting shadows over her dreams. She tossed and turned in her sleep, entangled in the ghostly remnants of the night's terrifying events. She didn't realize it, but she screamed in her sleep: her cry echoed in the silent castle through the walls and hallways, reaching the library room and even the secret hideout where Henri was.

Chapter Seventeen

Henri and His Young Victim

Meanwhile, in his concealed hideout, Henri stirred from his slumber, his senses alert to faint, distant sounds that had roused him from his sleep. The abrupt awakening sent a jolt of adrenaline through his veins as he sat up, bewildered and disoriented. The question gnawed at him: What had disturbed his peaceful repose in this hidden refuge?

There should not be anyone in the castle. However, he was sure he heard a voice crying.

Henri rose from his bed, his vampiric senses on high alert, as he glided through the shadows of his sanctuary. The mysterious cries that had pierced his slumber still echoed in his mind, sending a shiver down his spine.

He entered the library, his eyes scanning the dimly lit room with caution. The silence was oppressive, heavy with the weight of unknown dangers. His acute hearing, honed by his newfound vampiric powers, strained to pinpoint the source of the disturbance.

The sound came from upstairs.

Henri's unease grew as he crept toward the bed chamber. Who breached his sanctuary?

He pushed open the door, and his gaze fell upon the young woman, her slender form sprawled across his parents' bed. The same woman he had left behind, her blood still warm on his lips.

A chill ran down Henri's spine. How did she find him?

Her sleep was tumultuous, her face contorted in anguish. Nightmares ravaged her mind.

Henri's concern deepened, but alarm soon took over. Was she alone? Sent to infiltrate his refuge?

He cleared his throat to rouse her, but she didn't stir. Reluctantly, he shook her shoulder, his eyes locked on the red marks on her neck. But his worry soon gave way to alarm. What if she wasn't alone? What if she was a pawn in a larger game, sent to infiltrate his refuge?

Henri's eyes scanned the room, searching for hidden dangers. His fangs lengthened, ready to defend his sanctuary.

What did this woman want from him

Why had she followed him? Did she know what he was?

Henri cleared his throat to wake her up, but she didn't. Thus, he had no choice but to go next to her and shake her on the shoulder gently. While doing that, he saw the red marks he had left on her white neck, now swollen. He still felt the urge to suck more blood from her, but he tried his best to resist it.

The sudden disturbance stirred the woman from her unsettling dreams, causing her to startle awake. The woman's eyelids fluttered open, and their gazes met in the darkness. Henri's heart skipped a beat Her eyes, wide with surprise and apprehension, locked onto the unexpected figure before her, and she instinctively placed a trembling hand over her chest. You! You did this to me," she accused, her voice laced with anger and fear.

Henri furrowed his brow. "Excuse me, mademoiselle. What are you talking about, and why are you in my castle?"

Her gaze remained fixed on him. "I recognized your face. You're the heir to this place."

Henri acknowledged her observation with a slight bow. "I am Henri D'Ardent. Please, tell me what you're talking about."

The young woman's anger flared anew. "They banished me from the village... declared me demon spawn after seeing the marks on my neck."

Henri sighed remorsefully. "I'm sorry. The marks will heal. You won't be a demon or anything like that."

He sat beside her, explaining, "I'm a vampire, a night creature. I sleep daytime and move nighttime." He gestured toward the bruises. "I only took a little blood. If I had taken more, you would have become like me."

The woman's eyes widened. "A vampire."

Henri nodded, his gaze locked on hers. "Yes. But don't worry. You're safe now."

The woman's hand lingered on her neck, her touch tracing the teeth marks. Henri's heart skipped a beat, his thoughts torn between guilt and fascination.

Henri said, "Please, tell me your name."

The young woman replied, "Adele Morel. My father is the innkeeper in town." She furrowed her eyebrows as she recalled that she would never see her father again. "You must help me, Henri D'Ardent," she demanded, glaring at him and crossing her arms in front of her.

"Adele," Henri repeated. "It's a nice name." He paused and stared at her. "I don't have much money, and the little I have, I will need to start a new life. I can't stay here because, just like you, the town folk will recognize me sooner or later. I just came here to grab whatever was left and then leave."

"Where will you go?"

"Across the sea." Henri kept his eyes on Adele.

"Take me with you." Adele's plea hung in the air, a desperate request that revealed her fear of solitude in a world teeming with uncertainty, even if it meant seeking refuge with a vampire. "I can't stay here, and you will need company."

Henri, grappling with his own vampire nature and its inherent dangers to humans, hesitated before responding, his gaze fixed on her vulnerable neck. "I can't be with a human," he asserted. "I'm a danger to you, Adele. You know that."

Adele, undeterred by his declaration, pressed on. "If you sleep during the daytime, you will need someone to watch over you while you're dormant," she reasoned. "You won't survive without assistance from a human."

Henri's thoughts raced as he considered her words. She had a point. If he were to embark on a journey to find a ship bound for the new continent and reunite with his coven, he would need to traverse the treacherous daylight hours. He would have to stay in the dark, and someone would have to watch over his body so it would not be exposed to sunlight. He could hibernate during the long trip like Joliette, his queen, had planned to. He hadn't tried hibernation, but he hoped it was something all vampires would instinctively know how to do.

Adele's offer was reasonable. The world was full of perilous uncertainties, but perhaps, in each other, they could find the companionship and support they both desperately needed.

Henri nodded. "You would have to guard me in the daytime. When we reach our destination, I will give you the rest of the money I have left, and you could start your new life there," he said, keeping his eyes locked with Adele's eyes. "How would that deal sound to you?"

Adele considered it for a moment and then lifted her chin. "Yes, I will help you to travel there. I will need more clothes to pass as an aristocrat. I can't look like a servant girl if I must take care of your body during the trip. It would be more believable if I'm an aristocratic lady traveling to the new continent." She frowned as she thought about the deal some more. "We would have to hide your body in a coffin, I guess. We could say that you are my father that I have promised to bury in the new country." She lifted her eyes and met Henri's. "I think it will work. What do you think?"

"Sounds good to me," Henri replied. He extended his hand, and Adele grabbed it and shook it, smiling.

Henri gave Adele some money to buy a luxurious coffin. He didn't plan to stay in a wooden box with no pillows and cushioning for months. She was also tasked to find a ship for them to travel across the sea to the new continent.

However, they both knew that she couldn't go out flashing money in a servant's dress and thus, Henri took her to try some of her mother's dresses, which the looters had not found as they were in a hidden room. The entry to that room was hidden behind a wallpaper-covered panel that opened by pressing a rose next to the doorway.

After going through the clothes, Adele noticed that she didn't have to make hardly any changes to them. She was skinny, and the dresses she chose would fit her nicely.

For her shopping trip, she chose an elaborate gown with puffed sleeves, intricate embroidery, lace, and luxurious layers of silk fabric cascaded down in a flowing manner, creating a regal appearance. The silhouette of her dress featured a fitted bodice with a low neckline, accentuating the elegance of her figure. The waistline was high, just below the bust, which was distinctive of the empire style. The dress was adorned with bows, ribbons, and floral decorations.

Henri assessed her look with the scrunched forehead. "The dress looks good on you, Adele. You will also need a wig and a fan like all the aristocrats use these days." He pointed at the dresser where his mother's powdered wigs were left. "And you better pick up matching shoes. I'm sure there's plenty of those in the closet over there."

He gestured toward the large wooden closet, and when Adele went to open it, she found rows of silk shoes. They were narrow for her feet, but the material was stretchy, so she tried them on. "I think these will do," she commented after walking with the shoes for a moment.

After dressing, she twirled around and asked, "What do you think? Will they believe me to be an aristocratic lady?"

"Yes, they will. We won't go to Paris or anywhere near where the revolution is hunting the aristocrats. We'll head directly to Italy and try to find a ship there.

My father's carriage is still here, but we don't have any horses. That's your next task after the coffin. Bring us some horses. And I can drive us at night, and we can rest in the daytime. Only, I will need complete darkness. Thus, the coffin would be useful to have first," said, and his eyes veered to the pile of clothes. "Put aside the darker clothes. You will need those for the trip across the sea if you plan to tell everyone you're in mourning and that the coffin contains your recently deceased father."

Adele nodded and did as he told her to do. She found five dresses in darker colors, made of fine materials and decorated with pearls and beads. She picked out hats and shoes for those dresses while Henri took his father's clothes and packed them in a trunk. "I will need a change of clothes too." He gestured at the other trunk. "Pack your dresses and accessories in that one."

When their clothes were packed, Adele glanced at him. "This is going to be a real adventure. I never thought I would have these kinds of fine dresses and travel across the sea. I'm grateful for this opportunity even if it will take me away from my village where I have lived all my life."

"No need to thank me, Adele. I was the one who put you in this position. However, we both will benefit from this collaboration. You will get a new life, and I will have a chance to find my creator." His eyes looked sad when he thought about the vampire coven that had left ahead of him. Nevertheless, even if he were presented with the opportunity to make an alternate decision, he remained steadfast in his choice. The key factor behind his past decision was the need to assess his inheritance's remnants and secure the essential funds required to embark on a fresh chapter in a new country. Money would open doors for him. Nothing was ever free.

Facing Henri, she said, "I want you to know that you can trust me. I have nowhere to go. I will help you to cross the sea, and when we get there, you will give me enough money to start a new life. I want a house, servants, clothes, and money to live so I can find a husband and have a family."

Henri nodded. "Agreed." He hadn't told her he had lied when he mentioned to her earlier that he had only a little money left. He also had gemstones and valuable necklaces that had belonged to his family for decades. He could sell them, which would be enough for both of them to start over on the new continent. He recalled that Adele's father was the innkeeper. "Do you wish to say goodbye to your father?"

"No, the villagers won't let me enter the village," Adele recounted, her eyes veiled in shadows as the painful memory of abandonment lingered in her gaze.

"It's daytime now. I would suggest you leave the castle and find horses for our carriage. I wouldn't recommend getting them from your village. You could walk to the next one and get two horses from there. I will give you some gold coins." Henri put his hand in his pocket and pulled out two *Louis d'ors*—gold coins featuring the image of the reigning monarch Louis XVI in 1789. Henri handed them to Adele. "These are of high value. You probably need only one to buy two horses. If they have a good carriage there, then take that too. It will be easier for you to travel back. Besides, it might be better if we don't use the carriage left here because it has my family crest on the doors. Someone might recognize it."

Adele nodded. "I will leave as soon as I change clothes."

Henri shook his head. "No, don't change everything. Take a simple dress from the closet, and wear that. It will make you look like a servant of a wealthy family looking for a carriage. They will more likely sell it to you at a reasonable price. If you go there wearing the dress you had before, they won't believe you."

"That sounds good." She was about to leave Henri, when something came to her mind." I have one question," she started.

"Yes, what is it?" Henri raised his eyebrows.

"When we leave this country and start a new life in the new continent, then how do we communicate?"

Henri realized how different their past and their education was. Like all the noble heirs, he was home-schooled from a young age by a tutor who focused on preparing him for inheritance. His education included learning about their duties and roles, , behavior and manners, diplomacy, fencing, riding, and how to run the estate, he also learned English and Italy as part of his tutoring. He smiled and replied,

"I've studied English, and I can teach you during our trip. You don't need to know all the words, just enough to get by," Henri said adding. "You'll learn more over time."

"Thank you," Adele replied to him smiling back.

Chapter Eighteen

Adele (POV)

A dele left Henri's castle, heading across the vineyard and, thus, avoiding prying eyes. She crossed the fields and continued toward the next village, where she knew some villagers. Her banishment from her own village was a recent event, and she speculated that the news might not have reached this neighboring community just yet. She had covered her bruised neck with a scarf so she wouldn't be chased away from the next town.

Under the scorching rays of the hot sun, Adele pressed on, armed with a bottle of water that provided a momentary reprieve when she reached the summit of a hill. From this elevated vantage point, she cast her gaze down to the valley below, where her next destination awaited.

Taking a brief respite, she gathered her thoughts and energies before descending into the town. As Adele entered the main road, her focus shifted to finding a stable. She believed that the stable would be the ideal location to procure two horses and a new carriage for their upcoming journey. When her eyes found a sign advertising stable, she headed that way.

A middle-aged man stood there wearing a leather vest and baggy black pants.

"Excuse me, sir," Adele said, stopping by the staple's doorway. When the man turned and greeted her, "Good morning, miss. How can I help you?"

"I'm looking for a carriage and two horses." Adele said and added, "Not for me, but my master's carriage wheel was broken, and we are on a tight traveling schedule, and we won't have time to wait for the repair, so he sent me here to acquire another one. He's resting in a nearby village." When the man looked suspicious, Adele reached out to her pocket and showed one gold coin. "He gave me this coin to pay for your services."

"Sure, I can help you." With a measured nod, the man willingly assisted the young woman. As he observed her, a conviction settled within him, solidifying his belief that she was a servant in the employ of a noble family, seeking refuge from the tumultuous grip of the revolution. Disturbed by the unsettling rumors emanating from the capital city, he couldn't shake off the haunting tales of the merciless guillotine, the grim apparatus that had claimed the lives of countless aristocrats, one after the other.

The echoes of the revolutionists' march, leading the elite to their tragic demise, reverberated not only within the confines of Paris but also in the surrounding areas. Fueled by a sense of empathy and a desire to shield this young woman and the family she served from the impending danger, the stable owner took Adele to the back of the stables and showed her a nice black carriage and two black horses. "Would this be suitable?"

"It looks perfect." Adele smiled at him.

Responding to her sincerity, the stable owner took charge, orchestrating the arrangement of the horses in front of the waiting carriage. As the equine duo stood poised for motion, he handed the reins to Adele, guiding her up to the elevated seat in front of the carriage. Positioned at the reins, she received a brief tutorial on the fundamentals of carriage driving.

With practical instructions, the stable owner imparted the basic principles of horse-guiding. "You guide the horses with the reins," he explained, emphasizing the pivotal role of the leather reins in controlling the carriage. "Pull them if you want to stop; otherwise, just let the reins loose so they will run toward the direction you want." The intricacies unfolded as he continued, "Pull more on the left, and they will turn that way," offering Adele a crash course in the art of steering the carriage through the subtleties of rein manipulation. Adele was grateful for this impromptu driving lesson. Now she didn't have to find anyone else to manage the carriage for them.

"Sounds simple enough," Adele said. "Thank you for your assistance, sir."

Before she left, she asked, "Is there an undertaker in this village? My father died recently, and I'm looking for a nice coffin for him."

Responding with empathy, the stable owner provided her with directions to the undertaker's shop, understanding the gravity of her request. Adele followed the stable owner's instructions and arrived at the undertaker's establishment. Fortuitously, the undertaker was present at his residence, and he had a ready-made coffin available. Though it might not have been an extravagant or ornate creation, Adele deemed it fitting and asked, "Could I possibly buy that coffin for my father's final resting place, sir?" And when the undertaker saw the gold coin she had, he was eager to sell her the coffin.

The undertaker carefully carried the chosen coffin to the awaiting carriage. He carefully secured it atop the carriage, ensuring a dignified travel for her father's final resting place. She left the village and headed back to Henri's castle. The trip went much faster this time than when she was walking, and she arrived at the castle just after noon. She knew Henri would still be slumbering in the dark, so she took the carriage inside the stables so that no outsider would see them and went back inside. Next, she decided to carry the trunks in the carriage. They would be ready to go when Henri awakens.

Once the trunks were securely fastened at the rear of the carriage, Adele's awareness turned to the gnawing hunger that had quietly crept upon her. Realizing that many hours had elapsed since her last meal, she decided to address her growling belly before it was time to go check up on Henri.

Stepping into the kitchen, Adele was met with a scene of disarray, evidence of the chaos left behind by the looters who had ravaged the place. Undeterred, she resolved to take matters into her own hands and ventured outside in search of sustenance. Though weathered by the turmoil, the castle's vegetable and herb garden offered hope. Surveying the garden's offerings, Adele gathered potatoes, beets, carrots, and tomatoes, salvaging what she could. To complement these vegetables, she discovered a collection of herbs that had miraculously escaped the pillaging. Armed with this humble bounty, Adele returned to the kitchen, determined to prepare a vegetable soup for herself, combining the retrieved ingredients into a cauldron. The aroma of the simmering concoction filled the air. When the soup was ready, she ate two bowls of it fast.

Anticipating their departure from the castle, Adele couldn't shake the awareness that Henri, driven by his vampiric instincts, might seek out an innocent bystander for sustenance along the way. Contemplating the journey ahead, she recognized the imperative of negotiating a pit stop, preferably at a tavern, where she could partake in a meal herself.

Adele leaned back in her chair and thought about the uncertainties looming on their path. Her financial resources, primarily derived from the undertaker who hadn't accepted a full gold coin but had returned smaller denominations, comprised her current monetary holdings.

As she weighed the meager contents of her purse, Adele hoped that Henri might possess more gold coins. She didn't know how much Henri had, but she hoped he had enough because there would always be unforeseen costs and then they had no idea how much a cabin on a ship would cost She was acutely aware that the road ahead would demand more than just resilience and resourcefulness—it would require a delicate balance of pragmatism and cunning. They had to avoid the revolutionists, the Jacobins, and their supporters while traveling to Italy. When they arrived at their destination, she would be the one negotiating the cabin for her and the coffin which would contain Henri's body. She knew she shouldn't trust anyone because Henri's life was at stake, and not just his, but her future too. She had nowhere to go if something happened to Henri because the only life, she knew so far was the village from which she'd been exiled.

Chapter Nineteen

Henri D'Ardent and Adele Travel To Italy

W hen Henri D'Ardent awoke, he discovered Adele dozing off near his cot. Pangs of hunger gnawed at him, compelling him to distance himself from Adele, lest her tempting, pulsating veins filled with delicious red blood become an irresistible allure. Quietly slipping away, he shifted into a bat and soared into the inky black sky heading to the nearest village. Perched atop a roof, he scoured the surroundings for his next suitable prey.

In a short span, his keen eyes spotted an inebriated man emerging from a tavern, sauntering toward the alley adjacent to a house. *That's a good one,* Henri concluded. Swiftly, he glided through the air and landed noiselessly behind the man, assuming human form just as he landed on the ground. Seizing the unsuspecting victim, Henri sank his teeth into the man's neck, indulging in the luscious blood that flowed within. Henri refrained from draining his victims entirely to avoid transforming them into the undead, like himself. When he was done, he returned to his bat form and flew back to the castle. It was time to leave this area forever.

Adele was awake and waiting for him in the hallway. She knew immediately why Henri had left but didn't ask any questions. "The carriage is ready. We should go."

Henri nodded and glimpsed back toward the stables and saw a black carriage with a coffin on top of it.

"Looks good. Let me pick up the last items from the castle, and then we can go." Henri rushed upstairs and went to his father's study to take the jewelry, and gold left in the safe. He packed them in a small bag and returned outside. Adele was waiting by the carriage with the horses. She wore a simple dress, the same one that she had during the daytime. "You should change into a noblewoman's outfit. You're supposed to be delivering your father in the coffin," Henri commented.

"I can change my clothes inside the carriage." She opened the other trunk where the dresses were, pulled out a more lavish dark blue dress, and tossed it inside the carriage. Then she looked around and shivered. "I have a bad feeling. We should go now."

Henri nodded and climbed into the front seat. "I will drive. Climb inside."

Adele did as she was told, and Henri encouraged the horses to run fast.

Meanwhile, in the village from which Adele was banished, the villagers had gathered in the town square. "I've seen some lights flickering inside the count's estate," one man said.

"The count is gone. It can't be him, and the castle has been emptied of anything valuable. No one should be there." Jacques commented.

"The night devils might live there," another man said.

"I saw Pierre's daughter Adele driving a carriage today and going that way," another man added.

When the man who was bitten had woken up and went back to the tavern complaining about his neck. When the villagers saw what had happened to him, they chased him away and then gathered to discuss what to do. "We can't let this go on. This nighttime monster will pick up every one of us one by one. We have to attack before we are all like him," the tavern's owner said, slapping his hand on the table. "Take anything sharp that can be used to kill the monster and join me in the village square."

And the men went to their houses and gathered tools with them.

They had pitchforks and sharpened wooden spikes in their hands, and some carried lit torches. "We must kill the monster in the castle. He will take more of us if we don't," one of the villagers shouted.

"Kill the beast!" the others cried, and the mob started advancing toward the castle.

Their walking speed was not that fast, so when they finally arrived at the castle, it was already empty. The mob went inside, searching every room, but found no trace of the vampire anywhere.

Before leaving the castle, they set curtains on fire, leaving the burning building behind them as they returned to the village, angry but relieved that the beast was gone.

As Adele gazed out of the window, a distant glow on the horizon caught her attention from behind.

Instantly recognizing its nature, she knocked on the small window behind Henri's seat. When he opened it, she delivered the grim news, "They are burning down your castle."

Henri turned, his gaze shifting toward the horizon, and saw the flames and the dark smoke coming from the place that used to be his home. The initial spark of anger flashed in his eyes, soon replaced by profound sorrow. The remnants of his past were now engulfed in flames, leaving nothing for him to reclaim. Gritting his teeth, he redirected his focus to the road ahead. *This is the only path now*, he thought, determination setting in. *I have to find my coven and the woman who created me. That's my destiny. I have nothing left in this country.*

Chapter Twenty

The Attack

Henri drove the carriage like a madman, trying to get as much road behind him as he could. He didn't want the villagers to alert any Jacobins, telling them he was still alive, but a monster.

After a few hours of relentless driving, Henri orchestrated a quick switch of the horse team, ensuring a fresh set of steeds to propel the carriage forward on its hasten journey. He planned to ride all night long. He didn't need any immediate snack because the blood he had drunk was enough for him for now, and he would be sleeping in the coffin after sunrise.

Adele slept inside the carriage. She knew she would take the reins the next day while Henri was asleep, and then it would be her turn to continue taking them toward Italy's border.

The roads were in good condition. It had not rained much, so the horses and the carriage had no trouble going fast.

After six hours of travel, the carriage ventured into a forebodingly dark forest. Henri, undeterred, steered confidently into the shadows.

Four men clad in dark attire and their faces covered with a handkerchief obstructed the path, forcing Henri to bring the carriage to a halt. The horses, startled by the abrupt stop, whinnied and raised their front hooves in surprise. Adele woke up inside the carriage and glanced out the window, gasping when she saw the men ahead on the road.

There are too many of them! she thought panicked. *What can we do now? Is this the end of our journey?*

"Hand over all your valuables!" bellowed a tall man donned in a dark brown cape, tricorn hat, and long boots, brandishing a lengthy sword in his right hand. His companions were similarly attired, armed with daggers and swords.

With deliberate composure, Henri placed the reins aside on the bench. "You don't want to go down this path, gentlemen," he calmly stated, though his voice carried an undertone of threat to the men.

The leader of the robbers laughed. "Did you hear that, fellows?" he asked, turning to his companions, who chuckled and lifted their swords higher in the air, pointing them directly at Henri.

"I think this man wants to depart this life," the leader said ominously, taking a step forward.

"I will ask you to let us go if you want to keep your lives," Henri replied, looking icily at the leader. His calm manner made the robbers think twice.

The leader's eyes narrowed, his mind trying to figure out what Henri knew that they did not. Never had a victim defied them so brazenly. He scanned the darkness beyond the carriage, searching for hidden allies, but the shadows yielded no secrets.

His gaze snapped back to Henri, his voice dripping with malice. "I don't think we'll let you pass."

Henri's smile was a cold, calculated whisper. "You chose your fate."

In a blur of motion, Henri sprang onto the leader, his fangs bared. The leader's scream was silenced as Henri's teeth sank into his neck, draining the life from his veins.

The other bandits froze, paralyzed by horror, as Henri ravaged their leader. Then, with inhuman ferocity, he turned on the next, and the next, leaving a trail of crumpling bodies. His attacks were ferocious leaving the men unconscious, but he planned to drain them empty when he was done with the attackers.

The last robber decided to run. His shock turned into terror as he stumbled backward, tripping over the roots in his desperate bid to escape.

Three dead and one escaped, Henri thought. *That was enough.* His chest heaved with exertion, his eyes blazing with fury.

Turning his burning gaze on the carriage, he gestured Adele to stay there. It was time to stock up with blood. Soon, Henri stood amidst the bodies, his fangs smeared with scarlet, blood dripping from his chin like a ghastly waterfall. He had finished with the leader, and he turned his eyes on the next bodies. With a dismissive snarl, Henri finished with the rest of bodies draining them from blood, and tossed the bodies aside, clearing a path for the carriage. He consumed all of their blood, exceeding his needs, because his intent was not to leave any survivors. By draining them completely, he ensured that these men would not rise again as vampires. With calculated brutality, he seized the final body, and the air was filled with the sickening crunch of shattering bones – a sound eerily reminiscent of snapping twigs. Demonstrating his supernatural strength, he hurled the lifeless form into the forest, casting it aside like rubbish, far from the road. The night air was heavy with the stench of death, and Henri's chest still heaved with the thrill of the hunt. He had killed, and the rush of power coursed through his veins like liquid fire. As the last body fell, Henri's gaze locked onto the darkness, his senses alert for any sign of pursuit. He did not hear anything. No one was threatening them. The last robber who had escaped had not returned with additional men. They were alone.

Adele had observed the scene from the carriage window and shivered when Henri glimpsed toward the carriage. "You know what I am," Henri commented, and Adele nodded and withdrew back inside. He calmed the horses, who were scared as they smelled the fresh blood. When that was done, he climbed into the front seat. He took the reins, and they continued their travel, and this time, no other robbers interrupted their trip for the rest of the night.

When the horizon turned red and yellow, Henri stopped the carriage in the woods and stepped down from the front seat. "I must go into the coffin now. It's your turn to continue driving ahead. Try to get as much road behind us as you can." He picked out a purse from his pocket and tossed it to Adele. "Use this money to get yourself some food and the new team of horses as soon as possible."

"Do you think we'll meet any other thieves?" Adele asked, climbing down the carriage. She had changed his attire to a noblewoman's dark blue dress and wore a white, powdered wig and a large hat with a dark veil in front.

"We might, but I don't think they will attack this carriage during the daytime. Just be careful. Some people might wonder why a woman like you is traveling alone, but you will have to tell them due to your father's illness and sudden death, you are on this journey by yourself, and you hope to reach your party in an hour. Keep the lie simple and try to sound convincing that you have a party that you will join soon and that they are just an hour ahead of you or something like that," Henri advised Adele.

Next, he grabbed the edge of the carriage's roof, hauled himself up, opened the coffin, and settled inside, pulling the coffin's lid tightly close. "I will know when the sun has set. You don't have to wake me."

Adele settled into the front seat, her fingers wrapping tightly around the reins as she urged the horses onward. Henri's final words echoed in her mind reminding her of the possible dangers that lay ahead.

As the morning light crept over the horizon, casting an eerie glow on the forest's dark heart, Adele's unease intensified. The shadows seemed to lengthen and twist, hiding unknown terrors.

Her heart pounded in her chest, every snap of a twig or rustle of leaves making her jump. She was alone now, vulnerable to the whims of fate, with no Henri to shield her.

The carriage rattled forward, its wheels creaking in rhythmic cadence. She glanced nervously over her shoulder, half-expecting robbers to return.

Henri's protection was gone while he was in deep slumber. Adele steeled herself, squaring her shoulders against the unknown dangers.

"I must do this," she muttered to herself, her voice barely audible over the carriage's commotion. "I must face whatever comes next, alone."

As Adele drove on, she couldn't shake off the chilling encounter with the thieves from her mind. She glanced back occasionally, half-expecting to see shadows lurking in the trees, but the forest remained eerily quiet. With each passing mile, her unease grew, but she pushed herself to focus on the road ahead.

Hours passed, and the sun climbed higher in the sky. Adele kept a vigilant eye on the surroundings, her nerves on edge. As the day wore on, she encountered a few travelers on the road, but they passed by without incident. She stuck to Henri's instructions, weaving her tale of a grieving daughter on a mission to reach her family's gathering.

Eventually, as the afternoon sun cast long shadows through the trees, Adele spied a small clearing ahead. She decided it was as good a spot as any to rest the horses and herself. Pulling the carriage to a stop, she climbed down from the front seat and tended to the horses, ensuring they were fed and watered.

Glancing back at the carriage, Adele's thoughts turned to Henri resting inside his coffin. She wondered what dreams or nightmares haunted him during the daylight hours. With a sigh, she retrieved the purse he had given her and set off into the forest, hoping to find a nearby village where she could procure fresh supplies and perhaps gather information about their route.

As Adele disappeared into the trees, the forest enveloped her in its silent embrace, leaving Henri alone in his coffin, shielded from the burning rays of the sun. Despite the tranquility surrounding him, his mind was far from at ease. Memories of his past, his creator, and what happened to him at Bastille haunted him in his slumber. His life as a cursed being worried him in his dreams. He had never thought about becoming a vampire, and yet, that was the fate he was given. He hadn't had any other choice but to take that or be decapitated. Yet, amidst the turmoil, flickers of hope and redemption danced at the edges of his consciousness. He knew he wasn't an evil being. His fate was given to him with no alternative.

***

As the sun dipped below the horizon, casting hues of orange and pink across the sky, Henri stirred from his slumber. With a sharp intake of breath, he pushed open the lid of the coffin and emerged into the cool evening air. His senses, heightened by his vampiric skills, surveyed the surroundings, searching for any signs of danger.

Adele is not here. She must have gone to the nearby village to eat before we continue, he thought.

Henri stepped down from the carriage and stretched his limbs, the stiffness of sleep dissipating with each movement. He cast a glance towards the forest, hoping to see Adele soon.

Minutes turned into hours as Henri waited, the solitude of the forest enveloping him once more. The rustle of leaves in the breeze and the distant calls of nocturnal creatures were the only sounds that echoed through the night.

Finally, just as darkness began to blanket the land in its entirety, Adele emerged from the shadows of the forest, a bundle of supplies in her arms. Relief flooded through Henri as he greeted her with a nod, grateful for her safe return.

Together, they replenished the carriage with provisions and prepared to continue their journey under the cover of night. With Henri at the reins once more and Adele by his side dozing off after having a meal, exhausted from the long day, they set off into the darkness, their path illuminated only by the pale glow of the moon overhead.

With no extra distraction, Henri rode the carriage ahead during the night, and they reached the border of Italy. He headed down the coastline to the harbor, where he hoped Adele could secure them a ship to travel across the ocean.

Chapter Twenty-One

In Italy

Henri had visited Italy only once as a child with his father. However, the state of the country was different now than back then when all the separate states competed with each other. Italy had recently unified into a country in 1861, and Henri hadn't been there since the previously separated states had decided to join together. He bet that this union had improved the trades and reduced the bickering and competition between the separate states now that they were all working together.

Henri felt a surge of both excitement and apprehension. Italy, with its rich history and vibrant culture, was a world away from the dangers they had left behind. Yet, the task ahead loomed dauntingly before them: Adele had to find passage across the ocean for both her and Henri while keeping their true nature hidden from prying eyes.

As the carriage rolled into the streets of a coastal village, which would be bustling in the daytime, no other creatures were awake but mice and stray cats lurking in the shadows of dark alleys.

When the first rays of sun brightened the horizon, Henri stopped the carriage in an alley near the harbor, woke up Adele, and told her, "It's your turn to find the ship for us," and climbed into his coffin to sleep.

***

With Henri safely tucked away in his coffin, Adele set out into the awakening port city, her eyes scanning the array of ships moored along the docks. The salty tang of the sea filled her nostrils, mingling with the sounds of merchants haggling and sailors calling out to one another.

Where can I find a suitable ship? Her eyes met a harbor master's office, and she decided to go there to ask.

Adele's heart pounded with each step she took, the weight of responsibility heavy upon her shoulders. She knew that finding passage aboard a ship would not be easy, especially with Henri's nocturnal nature requiring special accommodation.

The harbor master was helpful, and he pointed out three ships and their captains who Adele could ask for a cabin for her and her dead father's coffin. All those ships were going across the ocean to the new continent. After hours of inquiry and negotiation, Adele finally found a captain called Roberts willing to take them aboard his vessel. The ship, the Tempest Lady, bound for distant shores across the ocean, offered the promise of a new beginning, and her captain was seasoned and had crossed the ocean many times.

With the arrangements made, Adele went to a near-by restaurant and had some dinner before she returned to their carriage, where Henri lay sleeping in his coffin, hidden from view amidst the shadows of an alleyway. It was already getting late in the evening, and the last rays of the sun were coloring the distant sky. Gently rousing him from his slumber, she relayed the news of their impending journey.

A glimmer of hope lit up Henri's eyes as he listened intently to Adele outlining their plans, his mind already racing with thoughts of the upcoming journey and what he would have to be prepared for. He knew his maker had told him that the vampires could be in deep slumber the whole time of the trip, but Henri wasn't that old vampire, and he couldn't be sure if he could stay asleep all the time. *Adele will have to procure me blood at some point,* he thought. But how? That was the problem. *Perhaps just mice and rats,* he thought, shivering as he wasn't keen on trying rodents' blood.

Henri returned to his coffin while Adele took over the reins and rode the carriage to the docks. With a mixture of excitement and trepidation, Adele boarded the vessel, and the two sailors helped to carry his father's coffin into her cabin. At first, they had questioned her decision, but Adele had been adamant.

"My father made me promise before he died that I will not leave his coffin out of my sight. I won't break that promise." She lied fluently to the sailors, and they believed her.

As the ship set sail, leaving the shores of Italy behind, Adele stood on the deck, her eyes staring at the distant horizon. Though the future was uncertain, she knew that she had made the right choice, trusting Henri. She would not have had any future in the small village if she had stayed behind.

Chapter Twenty-Two

The Journey Across The Ocean Starts

The sea breeze tousled Adele's hair as she watched the coastline of Italy shrink into the distance and disappear from her sight. Sighing, she turned around and returned to the cabin she shared with Henri's coffin. As Adele settled into the cabin, the rhythmic lapping of waves against the ship's hull enveloped her, a soothing melody she'd never experienced before. The tall ship's unfamiliar creaks and groans were strange. In the stillness, she let the ocean's serenade calm her nerves. Yet, beneath the peaceful surface, worries simmered. Their voyage across the vast expanse would be fraught with unknowns, and Henri's fragile state during the daytime weighed heavily on her mind. Would he remain dormant throughout their journey, or would the turbulent seas awaken him? Only time would tell, Adele thought, her eyes drifting toward the unknown horizon.

Inside the cabin, Henri lay in his coffin, his mind drifting between sleep and wakefulness. He was only in slumber and could hear the sounds outside of his his coffin. He tried to rest, but his mind was too restless. He knew they would need to be vigilant to keep his true nature hidden from the crew and passengers, but he also held onto the hope that their new life in the distant land would offer both of them the chance for a fresh start.

Adele and Henri settled into a routine aboard the vessel as the first week passed and the ship sailed farther from the familiar shores. Adele spent her days exploring the ship, getting to know the crew, and ensuring that Henri's slumber was not disturbed.

Meanwhile, Henri spent all his time in his coffin, resting and conserving his energy for the new world ahead. He found solace in the darkness, where he could escape the prying eyes of the crew and slip into the quiet embrace of sleep.

As the ship sailed further into the vast expanse of the ocean, dark clouds gathered on the horizon, obscuring the once-clear skies. Adele could sense the change in the air, the chill wind, and the moisture in it.

The crew's unease was palpable as whispers of an impending storm spread throughout the ship. Frantic activity ensued as sailors rushed to prepare for the tempest, adjusting sails and securing cargo in a desperate attempt to outrun the looming danger. With grim determination, they worked tirelessly to batten down the hatches and secure the ship, ready to face whatever challenges the tumultuous sea had in store.

Despite Captain Robert's commands to push the ship to its limits, the storm clouds seemed to move with an unnatural swiftness, racing ahead of the vessel like a relentless foe. No matter how the crew strained against the wind and waves, the impending tempest closed in with an ominous inevitability.

Word spread quickly among the crew that a storm was brewing, and soon, the wind picked up, howling through the rigging with an ominous intensity. Waves surged against the hull, sending the ship pitching and rolling with each tumultuous swell.

Each gust of wind carried a foreboding, and the crew braced themselves for the onslaught of nature's fury. In the face of such overwhelming power, even the seasoned captain felt a twinge of doubt, knowing that they could only do so much against the might of the elements.

As the first drops of rain began to fall and the sky darkened with the approach of the storm, the captain and the crew steeled themselves for the battle ahead. "Go back inside the cabin, Miss," Captain Roberts ordered Adele.

Adele had used Henri's last name to get a better cabin on a ship. She obeyed the captain immediately as the waves tumbled the ship like it was just an acorn and not a sturdy tall ship.

Adele hurried back to the cabin, concern etched on her face as she realized the danger they faced. She found Henri lying in his coffin, his eyes closed in an uneasy slumber. With a sense of urgency, she tried to secure the coffin, but the violent motion of the ship made it nearly impossible to keep anything in place.

Suddenly, a massive wave crashed against the side of the ship, causing it to lean dangerously to one side. Adele stumbled and fell to the floor, her heart racing with fear. In the chaos that ensued, the lid of Henri's coffin flew open, revealing him lying inside, vulnerable to the elements.

Adele's heart clenched with panic as she reached out to close the coffin, but before she could act, a bolt of lightning split the sky, illuminating Henri's face in a stark, eerie light. His eyes fluttered open, confusion and alarm clouding his features as he struggled to comprehend the chaos unfolding around him.

With a surge of determination, Adele braced herself against the lurching of the ship and reached out to Henri, who grabbed her hand, pulling her close to him.

Chapter Twenty-Three

What the Vampire Wants

Adele's fists tightened against Henri's chest, and her eyes widened as she noticed the look in Henri's eyes. They were not gazing at her eyes, but her neck, the pulsing vein, and her breathing got ragged.

Shaking her head, Adele tried to pull herself free from the iron grip of Henri's arms, but he didn't let her go.

Henri pushed Adele's blond curls behind her back and stared at her neckline.

"Please, Henri, no..." Adele started, her lower teeth sinking into her bottom lip. Bad move, though, as that made Henri notice the luscious plump lips filled with red blood.

"Ah, Adele," he murmured, leaning closer to her long white neck where the vein pulsed so deliciously. His lips on her neck feel like a whisper of a kiss, not biting yet, but sensing her warm, soft skin and awaiting the right moment.

Adele's heart skipped.

Sucking in a breath, Adele swallowed hard, his closeness making her heart beat faster. She was trapped with a vampire in the cabin in a storm!

Henri lifted his hand, and his fingertips trailed down from Adele's cheek to her collarbone and to the ample view of her round breasts that were hidden by the laced bodice of the dark silk dress. "So alive..." he muttered, his eyes glassy, his breathing heavy. "Feels like velvet," he commented as his fingers caressed Adele's skin.

His stare got heavy, stripping Adele naked without even looking at her but gazing into her eyes. Adele inhaled quickly as a heady sensation grew deep in her stomach and settled between her legs.

The storm raged outside, but inside the cabin, the tension was high. Adele couldn't get up or move away from Henri's arms—not that she even wanted it now. Her stomach flipped as the ship lurched forward, pressing her even closer to Henri's chest. Henri's closeness felt magnetizing. His lips on her neck were something she vaguely remembered from the village when he had sucked in her blood for the first time. Shivering, she relaxed in his arms. This was what she had waited for and craved. She hadn't known it before and had not admitted it, but now she realized she wanted to be with Henri.

Heat flooded through Adele's body as she realized her thoughts and what they meant. She would have to give up her life as it was and join Henri in the vampire world. Henri lowered his hand on her thigh and grasped it tight.

Adele's body ignited, a flush spreading across her cheeks as warmth pooled within her. Her pulse quickened, beating in secret places. With a soft gasp, she grasped Henri's lapels, her fingers curling into the fabric. Instead of pushing him away, she drew him nearer, her body yielding to the spark between them.

Henri's lips hovered by her ear. "Are you sure? Are you ready?"

"Yes, please, Henri." Adele's voice was just a whisper.

"I'll be gentle," Henri replied, leaning closer to her neck and sinking his teeth into its softness.

Adele's lips parted and her eyes closed as she felt Henri's teeth breaking her skin, sucking her blood, and then she lost consciousness. She wasn't awake when Henri finished feeding. He lifted her into his arms and carried her onto the bed's soft mattress and silky sheets.

"Adele," Henri whispered.

When she opened her eyes, he said, "I drank only a little bit. You won't be a vampire – not yet."

Disappointment flashed in Adele's eyes when she heard that.

"I can't drink too much of your blood while we are on the ship. We need your cover as a mourning daughter taking care of her father's coffin. That's the most important for now." Henri patted her hair, but his eyes traveled along her body.

Adele's breathing hitched as she saw the darkness and the heat entering Henri's eyes. His hands trailed up Adele's legs, and he leaned closer, kissing her on the lips and down her neck while slowly opening her laced bodice and revealing her breasts. He rose above Adele, his knees placed between her thighs, his tall frame shading her. He looked hesitating as if asking Adele's permission.

Adele's gaze met his, and she whispered, "Yes, Henri, please."

Henri nodded, and he lowered himself on top of her and kissed her fiercely while his hands explored her young body.

His eyes locked into hers for a short time, and he said her name again, "Adele."

She whispered, "Henri."

He pulled up her skirts, thrust his hips forward, sliding inside Adele, and she cried as she felt him inside her. A warmth spread through her core.

"Adele, you're mine now and forever," Henri whispered in her ear.

A solitary tear fell down her cheek as she replied, "I'm yours."

Chapter Twenty-Four

The Tempest Lady

The Tempest Lady was sturdily built and cut through tumultuous waves under the night sky. Dark clouds swirled overhead, and the wind howled like a banshee. Even though the rain had stopped, the sea wasn't calm. Captain Roberts stood at the helm, his face determined, while the crew scrambled to secure the rigging and the sails. The ship pitched and rolled as monstrous waves crashed against her hull, wetting everything onboard.

Captain Roberts shouted over the roar of the storm, "Secure the sails! Prepare for a heavy gale!

The crew, clad in soaking wet clothes and gripping tightly to anything solid, worked feverishly to reef the sails. The ship lurched violently, causing several crew members to stumble, but they pressed on with gritted teeth. They couldn't stop working because that would be a catastrophe.

First Mate Rimini shouted a reply while struggling to maintain balance, "Aye, Captain! Reefing the sails now!"

As the crew wrestled with the sails, a massive wave loomed on the horizon, its crest frothing with fury. The crew watched in horror as it bore down on them like an avenging demon of the ocean.

Second Mate Jenkins shouted, pointing frantically at the approaching wave, "Grab something! Brace for impact!"

The enormous wave crashed against the Tempest Lady's side with deafening force, sending shivers down the masts and causing the deck to shudder beneath the crew's feet. The crew gripped desperately to whatever they could hold onto, their hearts pounding in their chests as they tried to ride out the wrath of the sea.

Captain Roberts shouted grimly, "Hold steady, lads! We'll weather this storm yet!"

Despite the chaos raging around them, the crew refused to yield to fear, or more likely, they knew that giving up would be the end of them, so they had to go on. With each passing moment, they demonstrated their mettle, their resilience forged in the crucible of the sea. They worked as one, united in purpose, trying to save their own lives as well as the ship's.

Thompson pointed. "Another one coming! Hold on to something."

Fear washed over the crew as they caught a glimpse of a wall of waves on the horizon. With renewed vigor, they redoubled their efforts, guiding the ship through the treacherous waters toward what they hoped would be safer seas.

While the crew battled with the storm, Adele was in her bed, feeling sick due to the rolling waves but also because Henri had taken her blood. She had a splitting headache, her throat felt dry, and she didn't feel like trying to get up.

Henri had returned to the coffin in case any crew members came to check up on her, but no one did.

After several hours passed, Adele started feeling better. She got up and pulled a scarf around her neck and shoulders so the fresh bite marks wouldn't show. Then she cracked the cabin door open, saw the wet deck, and felt the wind blowing hard. She needed something to eat, though, so she dared to go outside, only to be sent back to her cabin by the first mate. "I will ask the cook boy to bring you something from the galley. Stay in your cabin, miss."

Adele felt relieved. Her legs weren't that steady yet, and she gladly returned to her cabin.

It took half an hour before the galley boy knocked on the door. He had a small tray with some bread and stew on it and a bottle of wine. "Here you are, miss." He handed it to her, and Adele took the tray and closed the door behind her.

Setting the tray on the table, she tried to eat it, but her stomach went around, and she quickly rushed to the bathroom to vomit. Returning to the table, she tried again with better luck. She knew she had to eat and drink because losing blood would otherwise make her ill, and she couldn't afford that, not with Henri onboard.

Chapter Twenty-Five

The Storm and The Hunger

Adele had finally managed to keep some food in her stomach, and she lay down on the bed to sleep. She didn't know how long she had slept when she woke up to the ship tilting so violently that she almost fell off the bed and had to grab the bedpost quickly to avoid crashing to the floor.

When the ship had leveled again, she viewed the room, noticing Henri sitting in his coffin, his eyes on her. His look was filled with insatiable hunger. Not in a way that made Adele feel terrified, but rather tightening the muscles in the pit of her stomach and cause the blood rush in her veins and her pulse to hammer.

"I know," he whispered, his voice almost inaudible due to the howling of the wind outside, "I scare you. I wish I didn't. I know what I am. I know what I was before I was transformed into a vampire. This wasn't anything I wanted for my life. I wish you could understand the complexity; I crave blood, but I don't want to hurt you. I want to leave you alone, but I can't. I'm awake, and I need blood. I can't stop this hunger growing inside me. I know you can understand." He stood up, strolled next to the bed, and sat next to Adele. He raised his hand to her hair, then carefully brushed the loose strands away from her face. His eyes turned to the swollen black and blue bruise around last night's bite mark. They darkened, and a shadow crossed his face. He lifted his fingers and gently touched it.

Adele withdrew a bit. Her eyes were wide, and she only shook her head. "No, Henri. If you keep feeding yourself from me, taking more of my blood, I won't be able to finish this journey with you. I will either die or become a vampire. You will need me at the destination harbor. You need a human to help you. You can't drink more of my blood."

"I know that," he breathed his lips close to Adele's ear. "But I don't think I can stop myself. I've told you, the hunger for blood takes over, and I can't fight that. However," he added, "I think it's not only the hunger for your sweet blood that keeps me wanting you, dear Adele."

"The thirst for blood inside me isn't the only hunger I feel." He half-smiled when he continued, "I can't stop dreaming of your sweet body in my sleep. I can see your hair, your big eyes, your long eyelashes shadowing your cheeks, your soft skin, and I remember how you felt under me. How I felt inside you last night. I know you didn't have a choice, but ..." His fingers touched Adele's lips slightly, and she gasped, feeling the heat in between her legs.

"Henri," Adele whispered, her gaze meeting his dark eyes. She swallowed hard. "We need to solve the blood thirst first before we do anything else. I can't risk my life."

Henri's lips wandered across her cheek and lowered to her neck.

Inhaling sharply, she pulled away from Henri. "Listen, Henri. You must snap out of this thirst. You can't do this to us." It was the first time she addressed them as 'us.' She had not realized she thought of them as a couple, as an item. The fate had brought them together.

Henri stopped and stared at her, his eyes clearing from the darkness that had entered them. He stood up, brushed his hair back, and then walked to the window. Cursing quietly, Henri said, "Who will I use then?"

Chapter Twenty-Six

The Thirst for Blood

Henri stood by the window for another immeasurable moment before turning to face Adele again. Now, his eyes were completely clear. "What should *we* do?" He wanted to get Adele's opinion because Adele had been around the ship and knew the crew better. He knew that the only humans close enough were the crew members. However, realizing they were in a storm and all the men were required to help the captain, he didn't know who would be less critical for the ship. Thus, Adele had to decide who his next victim would be. And he agreed, it could not be Adele.

Henri's eyes bore on Adele, demanding an answer. "Who should be my victim?"

Shrugging, Adele wrung her hands in her lap. "I can't decide." She lifted her gaze, begging him not to ask her to select the next victim.

"You must. You know this ship and her crew. You've seen everyone onboard. Who is less valuable for this journey?" Henri asked, his voice gentle.

Sighing, Adele's eyes turned back to her hands in her lap. She tried to recall the crew members. A skinny boy's image came to Adele's mind. The galley helper who had brought her the tray. He would be easy to attack. "The galley boy."

"He will be my next victim. Where can I find him?" Henri waited for her answer impatiently. He knew he couldn't hold his thirst for blood for long now that he was awake. *Cursed storm*, he thought, *that keeps opening my coffin and shifting it from side to side in this cabin. I can't sleep in these turbulent conditions.*

"I think he's always in the galley. He sleeps there on top of the potato sacks," Adele replied, turning her gaze back at him. "He's just a boy, maybe twelve years old," she added, her voice trembling with guilt.

"His blood will be enough," Henri assured her. He lifted his arms and transformed into a bat. "Open the window for me and keep it open until I return. I won't be long."

Adele stood up, walked to the porthole window, and stood next to it while the bat flew through and disappeared into the darkness of the night. The wind blew in splashes of cold, salty seawater with every dip of the ship. Soon, Adele's face and the front of her dress were soaked just from staying close to the open porthole.

Henri circled the ship, looking for the galley. The gusts tried to push the bat further away from the vessel, and Henri had to fight to stay close by. He landed near the deck, hiding in the shadows, and peered through an open porthole, where he saw the galley and a boy sleeping on the back. *That's the cook's helper*, Henri thought.

He pushed aside the guilt he felt and flew inside, landing next to the boy and switching back to his human form. His fangs were in the boy's neck before he even woke up and could cry for help.

Outside, the winds howled fiercely, their mournful wail echoing through the stormy night, mixing with the shouts of the crew members. No one missed the galley boy as they had their hands full taking care of the ship so it wouldn't go over or wreck in the storm.

When Henri had drunk enough of the boy's blood, he left his limp body on the sacks, knowing that the boy wouldn't be the same again. What he was afraid of was that the boy would go through the transformation of becoming a vampire instead of dying of blood loss. Henri couldn't control his thirst for fresh blood, and he was quite sure that the boy might wake up as a vampire. Shrugging, he quickly morphed into a bat and returned to Adele's cabin.

Adele closed the window after the bat had entered and turned to face Henri, who transformed into a human. "It's done."

Chapter Twenty-Seven

Henri's Hunger

Henri stood by the window for another immeasurable moment before turning to face Adele again. Now, his eyes were completely clear. "What should *we* do?" He wanted to get Adele's opinion because Adele had been around the ship and knew the crew better. He knew that the only humans close enough were the crew members. However, realizing they were in a storm and all the men were required to help the captain, he didn't know who would be less critical for the ship. Thus, Adele had to decide who his next victim would be. And he agreed, it could not be Adele.

Henri's eyes bore on Adele, demanding an answer. "Who should be my victim?"

Shrugging, Adele wrung her hands in her lap. "I can't decide." She lifted her gaze, begging him not to ask her to select the next victim.

"You must. You know this ship and her crew. You've seen everyone onboard. Who is less valuable for this journey?" Henri asked, his voice gentle.

Sighing, Adele's eyes turned back to her hands in her lap. She tried to recall the crew members. A skinny boy's image came to Adele's mind. The galley helper who had brought her the tray. He would be easy to attack. "The galley boy."

"He will be my next victim. Where can I find him?" Henri waited for her answer impatiently. He knew he couldn't hold his thirst for blood for long now that he was awake. *Cursed storm*, he thought, *that keeps*

opening my coffin and shifting it from side to side in
this cabin. I can't sleep in these turbulent conditions.

"I think he's always in the galley. He sleeps there on
top of the potato sacks," Adele replied, turning her
gaze back at him. "He's just a boy, maybe twelve years
old," she added, her voice trembling with guilt.

"His blood will be enough," Henri assured her. He
lifted his arms and transformed into a bat. "Open the
window for me and keep it open until I return. I won't
be long."

Adele stood up, walked to the porthole window,
and stood next to it while the bat flew through and
disappeared into the darkness of the night. The wind
blew in splashes of cold, salty seawater with every dip
of the ship. Soon, Adele's face and the front of her
dress were soaked just from staying close to the open
porthole.

Henri circled the ship, looking for the galley. The gusts tried to push the bat further away from the vessel, and Henri had to fight to stay close by. He landed near the deck, hiding in the shadows, and peered through an open porthole, where he saw the galley and a boy sleeping on the back. *That's the cook's helper*, Henri thought.

He pushed aside the guilt he felt and flew inside, landing next to the boy and switching back to his human form. His fangs were in the boy's neck before he even woke up and could cry for help.

Outside, the winds howled fiercely, their mournful wail echoing through the stormy night, mixing with the shouts of the crew members. No one missed the galley boy as they had their hands full taking care of the ship so it wouldn't go over or wreck in the storm.

When Henri had drunk enough of the boy's blood, he left his limp body on the sacks, knowing that the boy wouldn't be the same again. What he was afraid of was that the boy would go through the transformation of becoming a vampire instead of dying of blood loss. Henri couldn't control his thirst for fresh blood, and he was quite sure that the boy might wake up as a vampire. Shrugging, he quickly morphed into a bat and returned to Adele's cabin.

Adele closed the window after the bat had entered and turned to face Henri, who transformed into a human. "It's done."

***

Henri pulled Adele closer and kissed her passionately, bruising her lips with his hard and hungry ones. His hands explored Adele's every curve. His lips moved from her plump mouth to her neck and then lower to her breasts, and he kissed the cleavage partly covered in lace, and he started opening the strings of the bodice with trembling, hurrying fingers. Finally, when he got his bodice open, he buried his face in between her round breasts, kissing and biting each on e.

Adele exhaled quickly when she felt his teeth on her skin, and her legs trembled. She didn't know why his bite felt as sensual as the gentle kisses and touches. Her insides tightened, and heat flooded between her legs. She moaned as Henri pushed her dress down to the floor, and she stepped out of it wearing only long stockings and linen chemise.

Henri pulled the chemise over Adele's head so that she was all but naked in front of him except for the dark stockings that reached just above her knees.

She shivered and tried to cover her breasts, but Henri pushed her hands away.

"You are so beautiful," he said, pulling her close to him and kissing her fiercely.

Lust clouded Adele's mind, and she knew Henri was all that she wanted, all she had ever wanted, but also knowing that this love was forbidden, impossible, and should not happen...

Henri took her into his arms and carried her into the bed, lying on top of her.

Adele laid on her back and unbuttoned Henri's shirt quickly. Then, she pushed the fabric aside to feel his cool skin against her skin.

Henri's eyes looked bottomless and dark when he lifted his gaze from between her breasts and met her eyes. He let his hands follow each curve of her body until his fingers went between her thighs, and his touch made Adele gasp.

Closing her eyes, Adele dug her nails into his neck, pushing her body closer to his. She moaned as Henri's fingers played with the hot, wet area between her legs for a while before adjusting his position on top of her.

Gasping, Adele's eyes widened when Henri pushed himself into her and started rocking. Adele squeezed her eyes closed and moaned while Henri continued until his body jerked against hers and then went still. He laid on top of her for a while and then rolled over to lay next to her.

Adele's mind was busy. *Should I say something? Should I ask about the future? I can't have him, because he's a nobleman and also a vampire, and I'm just an innkeeper's daughter*, she thought, eyes closed. *I shouldn't give myself to him like this. I know this is a sin. I will never get a husband when they find out that I've been with another man,* she worried. *Although I can always invent a husband who had died in the old country. No one can needs to find about Henri. I don't have to tell anyone I was with a vampire.*

Henri turned and leaned on his elbow, looking at her with an unreadable expression on his face. He pushed a strand of her hair behind her ear. "What are you thinking, Adele?"

"About my future, or if I have any," she replied truthfully.

"You will have a great future. I will make sure of it. You won't be a servant anymore. You'll be a lady in the new country." Henri's voice was stern.

Adele blinked. "What if... What if I want to be with you?"

Henri's eyebrows furrowed. "You can't. I'm a vampire, and you are not."

"You can change that," Adele whispered, gazing at him.

"Why would you want to be a vampire, to live forever and only during the dark, never seeing the sun and daylight again?" Henri asked gently.

"Because I want to be with you," Adele replied, her voice shaking a bit.

Henri stood up and brushed his hair. "We shouldn't talk about this now." He walked back to the coffin and laid down there. "It will be daylight soon." He pulled the lid close behind him, leaving Adele staring at the coffin.

She realized Henri hadn't thought about being with her for longer than this journey, and he had not expected her to say what he had said. However, he had not said no either...

Chapter Twenty-Eight

The Galley Boy's Fate

Captain Roberts expected to have his dinner in his cabin, but when the galley boy didn't show up, he went to look for him.

When he entered the galley, his eyes met the cook staring at the body on the floor. The cook, a plump man with a balding head, turned to see who entered the galley and then gestured toward the boy.

"I found him lying there. His neck is bruised with two puncture marks," the cook explained. He was pale on his face. "He looks dead, but he's still breathing."

"This is the devil's work," Captain Roberts muttered as he kneeled next to the galley boy. "He's alive, but he'll no longer be human when he wakes up. I've seen it before. We have a monster among us now." Quickly, he straightened and looked around. His eyes darted around the kitchen, looking for a weapon to use. His eyes saw a metal hook by the windowsill. "Give me that," he ordered the cook, who went to the window, picked up the hook, and brought it to him.

Captain Roberts said a quiet prayer, lifted the hook in the air, and then, with all the force of his upper body, he lowered his arms, aiming the hook in the middle of the boy's chest.

The cook gasped when he saw this.

The boy's bones cracked, and his eyes opened wide, but almost no blood came from the mortal wound. His gaze changed from tormented to serene, and he sighed as he died on the floor.

"He's in peace now," the captain commented, pulling the hook away from the boy's body and leaving it on the floor. "What's done is done. We don't talk about this after this." He wrapped the empty potato sacks around the boy and ordered, "Grab his feet. We'll have to toss him over the board."

The cook did as he was told, and together, they carried the dead body outside and threw him into the tempestuous sea, where it disappeared.

The captain said a quiet prayer for the boy, and then he turned to face the cook and pulled him back into the galley. Inside, he said, "Don't mention this to anyone. We don't want to cause any rumors or fear among the crew."

The cook nodded, wiping his hands on the front of his shirt.

"We'll tell everyone that the boy stumbled over the board during the storm, and that was the end of him," Captain Roberts said. "Don't mention anything about the wounds on his neck."

The cook nodded.

"Now, give me my food. I have to go back to steer the ship soon and release the first mate. I can't stay long."

Gathering the plate with potatoes, stew, and a couple of slices of bread, the cook placed the plate on the table, and the captain sat down and ate there. He didn't usually eat in the galley, but this time, he decided to do so to save time.

"Give me some wine," Captain Roberts ordered.

The cook hurried to get a new bottle for him, opened it, and handed it to the captain. He drank from the bottle and then wiped his mouth with the back of his hand. "I needed this." He handed the bottle to the cook and said, "Have a drink. It will make you feel better."

The cook nodded, reached to grab the bottle, took a long sip of the wine, and then placed the bottle in front of the captain again. "Thanks, Captain."

"You did well not to leave the boy alone. I would not have wanted anyone to see the galley boy like that," Captain Roberts commented.

Chapter Twenty-Nine

Henri's Dilemma

A dele tossed and turned in her bed.

She moaned, "Henri."

Even through the walls of his coffin, Henri could hear her; however, he also sensed that it was daytime and that he shouldn't leave the coffin. The storm still raged outside, and the ship rocked up and down with every enormous wave. He wished the captain could reach calmer waters soon because this was intolerable.

Adele is asleep, dreaming, and calling my name, he mused. A tangle of emotions churned within him, as pleasure and trepidation entwined like the stormy waves they'd weathered. Henri's desire, once dormant, had been awakened by Adele's unexpected tenderness. Their sea-bound journey, meant to be a solemn passage, had become a catalyst for feelings he'd never anticipated. The tempest's fury had mirrored the turmoil within him, and he'd succumbed to Adele's captivating presence. Thinking about this trip, Henri wondered if his coven, led by Joliette, had experienced similar difficulties. *They left earlier, so maybe they avoided the stormy weather. I should have gone with them, but I wanted to get what belonged to m e*, Henri thought. *My estate and everything in there were destroyed by looters, but at least I got something out of that visit. I have money and jewelry to use when we get to the new country. I wouldn't have that if I had left with the coven.* His thoughts returned to his creator, Joliette, and he felt grateful. Being an immortal vampire was still better than being decapitated by guillotine. She hadn't been able to save many, but she did rescue a few aristocrats from La Monte-à-regret's deadly blade.

Adele's voice echoed in the room again, whispering Henri's name. "Henri."

No, I can't leave the coffin. She's just having a dream, Henri thought, trying to go to sleep. His active mind didn't allow him to do that. Adele's face and body emerged in his mind, and he could feel her body under him. *I want her,* Henri realized. *She's still a human, and I have to be careful. I can't turn her into a vampire, not yet, at least. Would I do it when we reach the destination?* Henri wondered. *Maybe I would if she wants it, too. What would Joliette say if I had turned another woman into a vampire? Does she have a say? She's my creator, but I would be Adele's creator. I don't know much about being a vampire,* Henri realized. *I don't know the rules and whatever else the vampires need to know to survive. I must find Joliette and the coven to learn more about vampire life.*

Henri listened to the blustery wind and then checked his inner clock. It was still afternoon, and he couldn't leave the coffin. *Adele will wake up soon*, he decided. *She needs food and wine to replenish the blood I sucked out of her.*

A sharp cry made Henri open his eyes. Adele! With his supernaturally sharp hearing, he listened to the sounds of the room. Adele moved around. *She's awake now,* Henri thought.

Wondering what Adele was doing, Henri kept his eyes open, staring at the coffin's lid.

He scratched it a bit to make Adele come closer.

"Henri? Are you awake?" Adele's quiet voice reverberated through the coffin's wall.

"Yes, I'm awake." Henri's voice sounded muffled to Adele's ears

"Why are you awake?"

"I can't sleep in this coffin. Too much turbulence," Henri replied. "Also, you called my name a while back. Are you well, Adele?"

Adele didn't reply immediately, thinking back to her dreams. Yes, she had dreamt of Henri's embrace and kissing him, but she had no idea she had said his name aloud. "I'm sorry if I woke you up."

"It was a surprise, that's all. You should go to the galley and get some sustenance," Henri commented.

Chapter Thirty

Henri's Predicament

As Adele moved around the cabin, Henri could discern the soft rustle of her muslin dress brushing against her form with each step, accompanied by the gentle tap-tap of her satin shoes upon the wooden planks of the cabin floor. Then came the creak of the door as it opened and closed, and Henri realized that Adele had left.

Closing his eyes, Henri started examining his feelings again. *Why do I care what happens to this peasant girl? I used her to satisfy his bloodlust in the village, caused her banishment, and then accepted her offer to help me get to the ship. Why do I care what will happen to her afterward?*

He realized he felt responsible for this woman! Maybe it was just some long-buried protective instinct—the strong for the weak, like when the aristocrats took care of their farm workers. He recalled how his father always made sure that the peasant families working for them were protected, had enough to eat, and made sure their families didn't suffer if something happened to the head of the household.

Henri didn't even know if other vampires cared for their victims, or was he different than the other vampires because of his past?

He hadn't thought about her when he had attacked her and sucked her blood, leaving her unconscious in the alley. She had been smart enough to figure out where he hid and found him. Or was that fate? Maybe they were meant to be together.

He tried to turn away his thoughts from Adele and empty his mind, but he couldn't. It was like he was obsessed with her. Groaning, he admitted the image of Adele's fair figure kept him awake and listening to the sounds around his coffin. Even the thoughts of her luscious lips and the taste of her mouth tightened his muscles, his stomach twisted, and his mouth felt dry like sandpaper. He wanted to taste her lips, kiss her soft skin between her breasts, and then move down between her legs to feel the moisture and lick her wetness between her legs. Groaning, he tried to remove the images of naked Adele wearing only the black stockings, but he couldn't.

Henri tried to shift his position inside his coffin, but it was too narrow. It wasn't made for living creatures but for the dead. Now, the coffin seemed more like his prison than his resting place. He felt like the walls of the coffin were becoming closer, and he felt tightness in his throat. *No, I can't be claustrophobic. I'm only imagining this because of Adele*, he thought, trying to clear his mind. He pressed his hands against the sides of the coffin, making sure that the walls didn't move, and it was only his mind playing tricks. Slowly, his breathing calmed down, and he relaxed.

The thoughts of Adele's body disturbed Henri in a way he didn't know was possible, not between a vampire and a human. It should not be happening, but it was. He wanted her; he had taken her to be his, and now she was his responsibility. What should he do with her? Keep her as his pet, or turn her into a vampire? He wasn't sure. He didn't even know if he wanted to ask Adele. He wanted to be sure of his wishes before letting Adele say what she wanted.

He heard the door creaking open.

Adele is back! was Henri's first thought, but then he realized the steps were heavier and thudded with every step. No, that wasn't Adele. The steps were too heavy. It was a man! Was he looking to steal something, or kill someone?

Chapter Thirty-One

The Stranger in The Cabin

As footsteps traversed from the doorway toward Henri's coffin, he tensed, apprehensive of the intruder's intentions. Was the man in search of the undead or perhaps some treasure hidden within Adele's cabin? Henri remained uncertain. Nonetheless, he prepared to spring forth should the visitor dare to lift the coffin's lid.

Henri heard the door creak once more.

"Pardon me, but are you seeking me?" Adele's voice drifted through the cabin, edged with a distinct note of annoyance towards the unwelcome intruder. She tried to sound like an aristocratic lady. However, Henri cringed at this, for Adele should not feign to be what she was not. It was possible that someone could discern her speech shifting from the manner of a common peasant to that of a noble lady.

The floorboards creaked again, indicating the man had turned to face Adele.

"Oh, it's thee, Captain Roberts!" Adele's tone shifted from anger to surprise, her voice now softer as she identified the intruder. "I did not recognize thee from behind," Adele continued calmly.

"I merely came to ensure all is well in thy cabin, Miss D'Ardent," the unfamiliar voice replied. Although he revealed nothing in his tone, Henri couldn't shake the suspicion lingering in his mind regarding the true motive behind the man's presence in Adele's cabin during her absence.

Henri waited for what would happen next.

"Did you know that our galley boy died last night?" Captain Roberts asked.

"I'm sorry to hear that." Adele paused and added, "I only saw him once or twice. The cook told me just now when I went to the galley to get some food that the boy was missing, assumed to be dead."

"Yes, we suspect he died during the storm. Possibly, a strong wave pulled him from the deck into the sea without anyone seeing it happen," Captain Roberts commented.

"Thank you for letting me know, Captain Roberts," Adele replied.

Henri listened intently to the conversation, pondering whether the captain's reason for entering the cabin was genuine or if another motive lurked behind his words.

Does he suspect foul play in the boy's demise? Henri recalled leaving the boy on the galley floor after satiating his thirst with the lad's blood. Though the boy hadn't been deceased at the time, Henri was certain he couldn't have survived the substantial loss of blood. The captain's assertion that a powerful wave swept the boy into the water seemed implausible. The galley boy was far too weakened to move anywhere after he had fulfilled his thirst.

No, the captain was lying. Henri was sure of it. He hoped that Adele would get rid of him soon. He didn't like this conversation or the captain's entering the cabin without Adele's permission.

"Is there anything else?" Adele inquired.

"No, I just wanted to be sure that everything was in order in your cabin," Captain Roberts responded. He stepped toward the coffin and Henri heard the floorboards creak with his steps. "I see that your father's coffin keeps moving across the floor. I can send some men to tie it down so it won't move, and the lid would stay closed in the storm."

"Thank you, Captain Roberts, but I am confident the storm shall soon pass, and with your expertise, we shall navigate to tranquil seas," Adele responded graciously, denying any offered help.

Excellent, Henri mused. *Dismiss the captain swiftly. I must converse with you.* He harbored the faint hope that Adele might somehow perceive his innermost thoughts, though he was well aware that she possessed no ability to read his mind or discern his desires.

"Well, I'll be going now. I hope you enjoy the rest of the journey onboard, Miss D'Ardent."

Heavy steps moved away from the coffin, heading toward the door. Henri held his breath, waiting to hear the door open and close before he lifted the lid.

Adele stood there in the middle of the floor, staring at the door. When she heard the lid opening, she turned to face Henri. "That was strange. What was the captain doing here while I was gone?"

"I believe he suspects that we had something to do with the death of the galley boy," Henri commented.

"You drank his blood last night. Was he dead after that?"

"Almost. I don't believe he could have walked anywhere from the galley after I finished with him," Henri commented, sitting in the coffin.

Chapter Thirty-Two

The Plan

Adele's gaze hardened as she processed Henri's words, a mixture of concern and determination evident in her expression. "If Captain Roberts suspects foul play, it could jeopardize everything," she murmured, pacing the cabin floor.

Henri nodded. "Indeed. We must tread carefully. The crew's trust is fragile, and any hint of suspicion could lead to dire consequences."

"Would they kill us?" Adele whispered, paling visibly.

"I don't know. Maybe. It depends on if they figure out that a vampire did the kill last night," Henri replied to Adele, looking grave.

Silence enveloped them, punctuated only by the distant sounds of the storm raging outside. Adele's mind raced, searching for a solution to their predicament. "We need to ensure that no evidence ties us to the boy's demise," she declared finally, her voice resolute. "We have no choice."

Henri's brow furrowed as he considered her words. "But how do we accomplish that? The boy's body was in the galley. That's where I left him, and based on Captain Robert's words, the body is no longer there. The story is that he stumbled over and ended up in the sea. It seemed to me that the good captain was covering my act for some reason. I wonder if he suspected who did the kill. Maybe he has even seen a vampire's handiwork before. I don't know..."

Adele's eyes gleamed with determination. "We need to move fast. Dispose of him discreetly. I trust the first and second mates to navigate the ship to its destination without delay."

"You want me to attack the captain and drink his blood next?"

Adele nodded. "Yes, you will need your dose of blood, and he's a healthy man. His blood will sustain you for a while."

Henri stared at her, impressed by Adele's quick thinking. "But where do we dispose of the body? We cannot simply cast it into the sea. Someone is bound to notice."

Adele's gaze flickered toward the window, where the storm raged with increasing ferocity. "The storm," she murmured. "It could be our salvation."

Understanding dawned on Henri as he grasped Adele's plan. "We wait until the storm reaches its peak," he said slowly. "Then, under the cover of darkness and chaos, we dispose of the body overboard."

Adele nodded, her eyes alight with determination. "We must act swiftly. The longer we delay, the greater the risk of discovery of who you are and where you're hiding."

With their course of action decided, Henri and Adele set about making the necessary preparations. They ready themselves for the dangerous task ahead. Henri was sure that if Captain Roberts suspected Henri of being an undead, he would be waiting for him, and he would not be an easy target like the galley boy was. However, Henri also knew that he could be swift, and no human could match the supernatural strength he had now as a vampire. Those were all his advantages.

"I'm not going until the middle of the night," Henri commented. "The captain will be tired by then and hopefully also asleep."

"Fine. I'll start eating. I won't go to sleep until you return," Adele replied, turning her eyes to the food tray she had brought with her from the galley. She pulled the food tray closer and started eating.

Henri didn't need that kind of sustenance. He knew now that he would have his thirst for blood sated later that night.

As the storm raged outside, Henri and Adele listened to the winds and waited for the later hours to start their plan.

Chapter Thirty-Three

The Captain's Demise

"Time to go." Henri opened his arms wide and transformed into a bat, just like Joliette had taught him to do.

Adele rushed to the porthole, opened it, and watched Henri fly through the window and into the dark sky. It was pouring rain, and the winds were blustery. She doubted anyone had noticed the window opening and the bat exiting her cabin window.

Flying around the ship, Henri tried to locate Captain Roberts and noticed that he wasn't steering the ship. Instead, his first mate was with the help of the second mate.

Excellent, he thought as he watched them navigating the ship and steering it past the enormous waves. In his opinion, they looked experienced. *I believe they can get us through the stormy waters and to our destination without the help of the captain.*

Next, he flew closer to the cabins to see if Captain Roberts was in his. He couldn't see through the window as a bat, so he quickly shifted back to his human form and then sneaked by the window to peak. And yes, there he was, lying on his cot. Henri watched him for a few more seconds and then went to the corridor leading to the cabins and quietly turned the knob, and entered the captain's cabin.

The captain had not moved.

Henri tiptoed across the floor toward the sleeping captain, ensuring he would not make any noise. He momentarily observed the captain's sleep, assessing the situation. With a silent sigh of relief, Henri concluded that the captain was deeply asleep, likely unaware of his presence.

Staring at the captain, his fangs came out, and he salivated. Lightning-fast, Henri leaned closer and held the captain by his shoulders, and before the captain could wake up from his slumber, Henri sunk his fangs into his throat, sucking the life away from him. It took only a minute to drain the captain's blood, and then Henri straightened, wiped his mouth from the excess blood, and looked around the cabin.

Captain Roberts was already dead, so he didn't need to worry about him.

Carefully, Henri scanned the cabin and strolled to his desk. He rummaged through the captain's belongings, searching for anything to help his cause. Nothing in the drawers. After a few moments of searching, Henri found a key ring hanging from a hook on the wall. Hastily, he grabbed it, thinking that it might be useful later on if he had to find something on the ship or lock some areas, and stuffed it in his pocket. He glanced at the captain, wondering whether he should take care of the body.

He decided that it was better to carry the body and drop him into the sea so that his crew members would not find out what had happened to him.

With ease, he grabbed the captain's lifeless body and made his way to the door, careful not to make a sound. He unlocked the door with practiced ease and slipped out into the corridor. It was easy for him to haul the body with the supernatural strength he had now as a vampire.

Carrying the captain's dead body, he walked through the corridor, making sure no one saw him. The ship was quiet in the middle of the night, and he didn't see anyone. Quickly, he pushed the body overboard, watching it disappear into the dark sea. *No one will know what happened to the captain,* he thought, relieved. Glancing around, he made sure no crew members were close, so he transformed into a bat again and flew back to Adele's cabin through the window.

Adele waited by the window and closed the port-hole as soon as Henri was in.

When she turned around, Henri had already trans-formed back into a human. "We don't have to worry about the captain anymore."

Chapter Thirty-Four

Adele and Henri

Henri brushed his hand down Adele's loose hair and pulled her closer to his body. He kissed her on her lips, and then his mouth moved toward her neckline.

Sighing, Adele surrendered to the passion. She pulled his head closer to her chest and enjoyed it as Henri slowly kissed her soft skin while opening her bodice and letting her dress fall. Now she wore only white chemise reaching to half-thigh and the stockings with silk shoes.

Adele swallowed hard as she noticed Henri's hungry gaze; however, she didn't resist, so Henri pulled the chemise over her head and then admired her young body.

Henri's gaze made Adele blush, but she didn't move. She stood there shaking, feeling the familiar throbbing between her legs.

Henri kissed her one more time on the mouth, cupping her plump breasts in his hands and fondling them, sucking one after the other before grabbing her in his arms. "I must have you, Adele," he said and lowered her into the bed. This time, he stared at her for a long time, his gaze following each curve of her body. He sat by the edge of the bed, his fingers skimming over her body, making butterflies flutter in her stomach. Henri's eyes flashed as they met hers.

Adele's heart seemed to beat so hard against her ribs that she was sure Henri would hear it, too.

Pulling her closer, Adele unbuckled his pants so that she could touch his cold skin. "You always feel so cool," she commented.

"Vampires don't have blood circulation," Henri replied, pulling off his shirt, kicking away his shoes, taking off his pants, and then positioning himself next to Adele. Her tongue licked her lips as she saw Henri's excitement clear in front of her before he descended over her, his muscular body covering hers. She blew out a shaky breath. She wanted him and recalled how she had felt the previous times when he had taken her. This time, she wanted to be active, and she let her hand touch Henri's shaft, feeling it, squeezing it, and moving her fingers up and down. This time, he moaned in pleasure. "Let me make you feel my love." He pulled away from her, and then his lips kissed her belly, moving downwards to the wet area between her legs, and he kissed her there, playing with his tongue and making Adele squirm in pleasure. After a while, Henri placed his knees between my thighs and then grabbed her by the hips, and then thrust his hips forward, gliding his shaft inside her. His eyes locked on hers, and he kept moving inside her.

Adele closed her eyes, moaning in pleasure. Her arms flew around his shoulders, and she held him tight against her until he collapsed on top of her, breathless and tired.

Their breaths mingled in the cabin's air as they lay there resting. The sounds of the ocean, the splashes of the waves, and the howling of the wind were the only ones piercing through the silence.

Adele's eyes were closed. She didn't even want to move a muscle. She felt completely relaxed and satisfied. *I don't want to think about tomorrow and what will happen to me*, she thought. *This is my life now. I can't change it even if I wanted to. The path was given to me when Henri drew my blood, and now I just have to make the best of the cards I was dealt with.*

Henri pondered the events that took place in the captain's cabin. He realized that in the world of vampires, survival often came at a steep price, one that sometimes demanded sacrifices that went against his moral compass. The insatiable need to drink blood, to protect himself and his kind, often clashed with his desire to uphold ethical standards. Despite his discomfort with taking a life, Henri understood the ruthless nature of his existence as a vampire. It was a constant battle between his taught societal values and the primal instincts ingrained within him as an immortal being.

Chapter Thirty-Five

Adele's Dreamworld

After the busy, tiring evening, Adele fell into a restless sleep after Henri went back to his c-offin. She dreamt of Henri and herself living together. In the dream, Adele found herself transported to a quaint farmhouse nestled amidst the rolling hills of colonial America. The kitchen was illuminated by the soft glow of candlelight, casting dancing shadows on the wooden beams above.

As Adele watched a maid knead the bread dough on the worn wooden table, a child's laughter filled the room, drawing her attention. She turned to see a four-year-old child who bore a striking resemblance to Henri, with similar dark curly hair and sparkling eyes.

"Momma, look what I found!" the child exclaimed, holding up a freshly picked wildflower with a grin.

Adele's heart swelled with warmth as she enveloped the child in a loving embrace, feeling a sense of maternal bliss wash over her. In this dream world, Henri was there, his presence silent. Adele didn't see him, but she sensed him or knew that he was close by.

However, soon, the dream changed into a nightmare.

In Adele's nightmare, the farmhouse suddenly became a place of desolation and terror, its once welcoming walls cloaked in cobwebs, and the light was replaced by shadows. The air was heavy with a sense of foreboding, and every creak of the floorboards echoed like a sinister whisper, inviting the monsters to find her and her child.

As Adele attempted to walk through the darkness, she was startled by a chilling laughter that seemed to emanate from the shadows behind her. Whirling around, she saw a child who bore a haunting resemblance to Henri, but with eyes that gleamed with an unsettling intensity.

"Momma, look what happened to me! Look what became of me," the child whispered, her voice sending shivers down Adele's spine. "Why did you let this happen to me?'

Adele's heart clenched with anguish as she reached out to the child, but she recoiled from her touch, her features contorted with hunger, and she opened her mouth, revealing bloody teeth. The house seemed to warp around them, its walls closing in like a prison.

Desperate to flee from the nightmarish child with blood-stained teeth, Adele raced through the twisting corridors, her footsteps reverberating in the hollow silence of the empty hallways. Despite her frantic efforts, she couldn't shake off the chilling presence of the child who pursued her.

Adele felt the oppressive weight of the child's malevolent laughter with each turn, clawing at her sanity as it echoed through the desolate rooms. The flickering candlelight cast elongated shadows that danced mockingly along the walls, heightening her dread.

As Adele's frantic flight through the dark corridors continued, she couldn't help but notice a peculiar detail. Glancing back at the wavering dance of the candlelight, she realized that only her own shadow stretched across the walls, devoid of any accompanying silhouette belonging to the child. A chill raced down Adele's spine as she processed this unsettling revelation. How could the child, so vivid and menacing in its presence, be without a shadow? Was it a ghost? Or a demon? Or something else? Adele didn't know in her dream. The absence of the child's shadow seemed to defy the natural order, filling Adele with terror.

With her heart hammering in her chest, Adele pushed herself to run faster, the rhythmic pounding of her footsteps echoing on the wooden floors. Yet, no matter how far she fled, she felt the mysterious child still followed her.

As Adele's panic reached a crescendo, she stumbled onto the floor, consumed by the suffocating grip of her terror. And in that moment of despair, she prayed for dawn to break and release her from the nightmare's grip, longing for the solace of waking from this harrowing ordeal.

In the depths of her terror, Adele cried out for Henri, praying for his presence to banish the terror that was about to consume her. But her pleas went unanswered, and she was left alone in the suffocating embrace of her nightmare.

When Adele finally awoke, her heart was still gripped by fear, and the memory of the nightmare lingered like a shadow. She clung to the hope that it was just a dream, but deep down, she knew that something in the dream was true; she just wasn't sure if she wanted to think about it, but not now. She lowered her hand over her belly...

What if I'm pregnant? Could I be pregnant?

Henri was a vampire, but Adele didn't know if the vampires could have children with humans.

Chapter Thirty-Six

Adele

At daybreak, Adele thought about all the folklore she had heard of the undead, the monsters that hunted humans and drew their blood after sunset. She had never heard of if these night creatures could have a child or that there could be a child vampire...

Could the child be born as a vampire, or would they evolve into something entirely distinct? Is there a chance for the child to be simply a normal human? She was confused and unsure.

I made love to him without even thinking twice... What if I'm pregnant? Can I be pregnant?

Sighing, she wished she had listened to more of the old folk tales to understand more what these vampires could do. She was unable to find answers to her recollections, but she decided to ask Henri about it upon his waking.

However, she realized something was different this morning. The ship sailed smoothly, and no more rocking or howling winds. She turned her gaze toward the porthole and noticed the sun shining outside.

The storm is over! she mused excitedly and quickly got dressed in her ankle-long black dress with a high collar to cover the marks on her neck. She twisted her long hair into a neat bun. She glimpsed Henri's coffin. The lid was closed, and nothing seemed to be amiss in the cabin. She knew Henri would be in slumber now that the ship wasn't climbing up the high waves and then crashing down.

The constant motion had been unexpected, and hopefully, the rest of the travel across the ocean will be easier, she thought.

Checking out her outfit one more time, she decided she was ready to leave the cabin and go outside on the deck. She unlocked the cabin door, closed it silently behind her, and then quickly headed to the galley for breakfast. Her footsteps echoed in the hallway.

In his sleep, Henri could discern the delicate rhythm of Adele's footsteps echoing through the ship's hallway. With a subtle shift, his consciousness edged closer to wakefulness, drawn by the familiarity of her presence. However, as he realized she was gone, he let himself fall back into a deeper slumber.

Meanwhile, Adele entered the galley. The ship's crew bustled about, their voices carrying a sense of nervousness. The discussion quieted when Adele entered the galley, and the gazes turned to her. The men looked nervous, even fearful.

Trying to look calm, Adele took a seat at a nearby table, her thoughts returning to the two murders: the galley boy and the captain. She guessed that the crew was now suspicious of the passengers: Adele and the coffin. Should she say something or just eat and leave the galley? She decided to do the latter. Her eyes darted around, and she saw the cook. "Could I have some breakfast, please?" she asked with a haughty tone as if she had not noticed the tense atmosphere in the galley.

The cook gave her a concerned glance and then went to fill a tray and brought it in front of her: a bowl of porridge, toast, and a glass of wine. Adele looked up at him and into his eyes, seeing the unasked question in them. "Thank you, this is enough." She started eating slowly, enjoying every bite.

The crew's eyes followed her every move. Eventually, they continued their breakfast, giving her a few suspicious glances. She ignored them.

However, when she had almost finished her meal, she heard the second mate commenting, "She can't be a monster. She is out in daylight and eating like a normal person."

"Something must have happened to the captain. He's missing. He wouldn't disappear like this. He never drank so much that he would fall overboard," the first mate added, giving Adele another stare.

Aha, they are aware that the captain is missing. Do they know about Vampires? Will they guess where he spends his daytime? Adele wondered. After finishing her breakfast, she left the kitchen and went out to walk around the deck in the sunshine. It felt heavenly to breathe in the fresh air and see the clear sky.

Chapter Thirty-Seven

At the Galley After Adele's Departure

First Mate Rimini's somber gaze trailed Adele's departure, then shifted to Second Mate Jenkins. "I reckon our visitor and that coffin are linked to the captain's disappearance," he grumbled, his brow furrowed with concern. With the captain gone, Rimini reluctantly shouldered his duties, though he harbored no joy in the prospect. Yet, he anticipated a promotion to captaincy once they reached their destination.

"You might be onto something," Second Mate Jenkins replied, taking a sip of water from his cup now that rainwater filled their barrels, reserving wine and cognac for the paying passengers and the absent captain.

The cook, having overheard, approached their table. "I don't know if the captain mentioned it, but the galley boy passed away the night before he vanished."

"How did he perish?" Rimini inquired, eyeing the cook who wiped his hands on his apron.

"I found him among the potato sacks, lifeless," the cook explained, a hint of fear in his eyes as he glanced toward the door to ensure their guests weren't eavesdropping. "Two puncture marks adorned his neck, surrounded by bruises. His skin was ashen, and there was little blood around the wounds."

"Captain Roberts examined the body," the cook added.

"And what became of him?" Rimini pressed.

"We wrapped him in sacks and cast him overboard during the storm," the cook said, a troubled frown creasing his brow. "The captain seemed concerned when he saw the wounds."

"Did he voice any suspicions?" Rimini inquired further.

Shaking his head, the cook replied, "Not to me. And now he's gone."

"The captain mentioned inspecting Miss D'Ardent's cabin and her father's coffin while she was away," Rimini recalled. "I'm certain he believed he'd find evidence there related to the galley boy's demise."

"It's baffling not knowing the captain's thoughts, especially now," Rimini exclaimed, frustration coloring his tone. "How can we uncover the killer if he keeps us in the dark?"

As the conversation unfolded, a tense atmosphere settled over the table, uncertainty pressing down on the crew. First Mate Rimini's mind raced, grappling with the pieces of the puzzle laid out before him. He glanced at the second mate, breaking the silence, asking, "What do you think we should do?"

Second Mate Jenkins's voice was tinged with unease. "We should search this ship and all the cabins and storage areas thoroughly and make sure Captain Robert's body is not stashed anywhere. If he was still alive, then he would have shown himself by now."

"You are right. We can't afford to be in the dark anymore. The storm has passed. We have a clear sky and calm waters, and we can reach the harbor in a few days... that is, if no one else disappears or dies. If we lose more men, then it will be difficult to handle the ship," the first mate replied. "We need to gather what information we can and piece together what happened to our captain."

Unbeknownst to Adele, while she savored the warmth of the sun and the boundless expanse of the sea, the crew silently conspired to investigate her cabin as well.

She stood on the deck, basking in the gentle caress of sunlight, her gaze drifting upward to the flawless expanse of cerulean sky, devoid of any trace of clouds. A wistful sigh escaped her lips as she longed for the entirety of their voyage to be blessed with such serene weather.

Lost in reverie, her thoughts inevitably turned to Henri, her companion, resting in peaceful repose within the confines of his coffin, nestled in the cabin below. She couldn't shake the melancholy that clung to her heart, a bittersweet reminder of their shared journey and the weight of her responsibilities. She had promised to help Henri when they reached the destination harbor, but she didn't know what to expect to find in the new country. What would become of her?

Chapter Thirty-Eight

The Search

The crew decided to comb through the ship deck by deck and look for the devil that could have caused the two deaths. First Mate Rimini led them down to the lower deck, leaving only a couple of men above the decks. Second Mate Jenkins was left to steer the ship, and a few crewmen were also there to help with the sails.

In a state of panic, the crew scrambled to arm themselves with anything they could find in the galley – knives, mostly, but some grabbed oars and heavy iron bars, their minds racing with the terrifying possibility of confronting an unknown threat. Fear gripped their hearts as they prepared to face the unknown, their makeshift weapons a meager defense against the sinister forces they believed were now lurking in the shadows of the lower decks. Every creak of the ship, every groan of the wooden hull, made them jump, their nerves stretched taut as they waited for the inevitable.

They scoured the hold, the darkest, most foreboding level of the ship, where the cargo and provisions were stored, but their frantic search yielded nothing out of the ordinary. The silence in the area seemed to mock them, heightening their anxiety with every passing moment. Undeterred, they pressed on and combed the cramped, dimly lit area between the decks, where the crew quarters and extra storage spaces were located. But, to their mounting dismay, they found nothing – no clue, no hint, no trace of anything threatening.

The men were now more relaxed. Maybe the death of their captain and the galley boy were just weird accidents...

Their search continued to the lower deck, where the galley and some crew quarters were located, and also nothing was found in those areas. The cook was obviously pleased that his working area was cleared and the devil wasn't hiding in the lower deck area. Next was the orlop deck, which was used for storage, maintenance, and access to the ship's hull. Nothing was out of the ordinary there, either.

All the men were now relaxed, even joking and chatting together. The only place left was the main deck and the cabins. First Mate Rimini raised his voice over the chattering men. "We must now go through the main deck and the cabins. If we don't find anything there, then we must admit that these two deaths were just accidents or natural deaths." He knew well that they were not. However, he couldn't say what had caused them because they had not found anything in any lower decks.

The captain's cabin was in disarray after the storm tossed items and documents on the floor. His bed was not made, and the cabin looked like the captain could walk in any time and settle on his chair to write a note into his captain's log. First Mate Rimini couldn't shake off the feeling that the captain's presence still lingered, potent and unmistakable. The pungent aroma of tobacco and sweat seemed to amplify his absence, making it hard to believe he had vanished without a trace.

Yet, despite scouring every deck from stem to stern, they had found no sign of him – neither alive nor dead. The mystery of his disappearance only deepened, leaving Rimini with a sense of unease and a lingering question: what had really happened to their captain? He believed what the cook had told him, but only partly. The galley boy could have contracted a disease and died. Many did due to malnutrition. However, Captain Roberts was a seasoned sailor. He wouldn't have accidentally fallen overboard or gotten sick without his closest mates not knowing about it.

No, the more he pondered, the more sure he was that something had killed the captain or he had stumbled into something mysterious. The ship had only one paying passenger, Miss D'Ardent. She had insisted that her dearly departed father's coffin be in the same cabin with her. She had claimed it was her father's last wish to travel across the ocean to the new continent with his daughter, and now she was fulfilling that dream. It didn't sound too strange, Rimini mused. However, that cabin was now the only place they hadn't searched through thoroughly.

Chapter Thirty-Nine

The Attack

When Adele returned from her walk on the deck, she was confronted by five crew members, their faces stern and foreboding. The first mate, Rimini, stepped forward, his voice cold and menacing.

"Miss, the captain has vanished, and we've scoured every inch of this ship from the depths of the lower decks to the bridge. Now, we're going to search this cabin, with or without your consent."

Adele's voice trembled slightly as she protested, "I assure you, Mr. Rimini, the captain is not in there."

Rimini sneered, his eyes glinting with intensity. "We'll take our chances. Step aside, miss." He gestured to the men behind him, who brandished their weapons with an air of hostility. Adele retreated from the door, her heart racing with fear.

"If you insist, Mr. Rimini," she stammered, her eyes fixed on the menacing crew.

Rimini's smile was cruel as he nodded to his men. "Oh, we insist."

With that, they pushed past Adele and stormed into the cabin, their weapons ready. Adele was left standing in the darkness, her heart pounding in her chest, wondering what horrors they might uncover... or unleash.

Inside the cabin, Henri lay in wait, his ears tuned to the conversation outside his coffin. He had been expecting this moment, his senses heightened with anticipation. As the door creaked open, he slowly lifted the lid of his coffin, his movements deliberate and calculated.

The captain's demise had been merely the beginning. Henri had known the crew would come for him eventually, and he had been lying in wait, his slumber a mere pretense. His eyes gleamed in the darkness, his heart racing with excitement. The moment of reckoning had finally arrived.

With a quiet, deliberate motion, Henri emerged from his coffin, his eyes fixed on the intruders. The air was heavy with tension as he prepared to strike, his fangs bared and ready. The five crew members had disturbed his rest, and now they would pay the price. The silence was palpable as Henri waited, poised to unleash his wrath upon the unsuspecting sailors.

A shape emerged from the shadows. Tall, gaunt, and impossibly pale, with eyes that glowed like embers in the dark. The vampire's gaze latched onto the sailors, and they felt a chill run down their spines.

At first, they tried to fight back. But the vampire was too strong, too fast. It moved among them with deadly precision, its fangs sinking into their necks like daggers. The sailors screamed and struggled, but it was no use. One by one, they fell to the deck, their bodies drained of life.

Only one man was left, First Mate Rimini. He cowered in the corner of the cabin, his eyes wide staring at the approaching vampire in terror.

Soon the creature loomed over him, its eyes burning with an unholy hunger. "Do as I ask, and I will spare you," Henri hissed at Rimini.

Rimini was as white as a ghost. He nodded. "Anything. Please, don't kill me."

"You will help us to get to our destination. I won't disturb you or the rest of the crew if you do that," Henri retorted.

"I will do that." Rimini's voice was barely audible. "We have just enough crew members left to take this ship to the harbor."

"And don't bother Miss D'Ardent. She's only working for me just like you are now," Henri added. His gaze turned somber. "I will return to my coffin now, but if I hear anything disturbing or that Miss D'Ardent has been treated badly, I will arise again."

First Mate Rimini nodded, relieved. He was left alive, surrounded by the bodies of his comrades. He knew that he had to do what the vampire asked. He had no choice.

Chapter Forty

Adele

Adele's gaze swept across the cabin, where the lifeless bodies of the crew members seemed to watch her with cold, dead eyes. The air was heavy with the stench of death. Her eyes landed on the coffin where Henri had retreated for the day, and a chill ran down her spine. As the bile rose in her throat, she fought to keep her breakfast down, pressing a trembling hand to her mouth. She closed her eyes, counting to ten in a desperate bid to calm her racing heart. When she opened them again, the scene before her seemed even more macabre.

I hope they don't become vampires like Henri, or we'll be in trouble. Not many crewmen are left, and then there's me, Adele thought, shivering. She had seen Henri kill the robbers in the forest before, so that part wasn't new to her, but she had never seen this many men killed lightning-fast.

In the forest, he killed three men, and the rest ran away. This time, he had let only one live. Why did he leave only one alive? Because this whole journey on this ship has been dangerous from the beginning, and with days of a storm rocking the ship, Henri hasn't been able to go to deep sleep and is now agitated? Adele had no idea.

How can Henri consume that much blood in such a short time? Adele wondered. *Can vampires drink that much blood and not feel full or sick? I guess they can.*

With a shudder, she forced herself to move, carefully stepping over the first body to avoid disturbing its gruesome pose. She couldn't bear the thought of staying in this ghastly slaughterhouse a moment longer.

I must get the rest of the crew to clean this cabin, she thought, her heart racing. *I can't stay here, surrounded by these dead bodies.*

When she got to the deck, the breeze caressed her face, and the smell of the ocean made her feel better. Determined, she walked to find the first mate. When she found him in the galley sitting and drinking, still looking pale and shocked, she sat across the table and crossed her hands on top of it. "I need you and other men to clear the cabin of the bodies before nightfall."

Rimini scoffed and continued drinking.

Adele's eyes narrowed, her gaze piercing as she issued a stern warning: "Defy me, and you'll suffer the consequences. I'm not making idle threats. You know exactly what will become of you if you disobey." Her firm tone and unyielding stare left no room for misinterpretation.

This time, Rimini turned his gaze at her and seeing that she was serious, his face turned ashen. "I'll let the men know," he muttered.

"Thank you," Adele said, rising slowly from her seat, as she didn't feel so good. She walked on the deck inhaling fresh air, opting to stay on deck rather than retreating to the cabin. The warm sunshine and gentle breeze brought a welcome sense of calm, soothing her queasy stomach and lifting her spirits.

As she stood on the deck, Adele's mind wandered to the changes unfolding within her body. She tenderly touched her stomach, and a mix of awe and trepidation washed over her. She had been avoiding the truth, but now, in the solitude of the deck, she confronted the astonishing reality: she was pregnant.

The thought of a new life growing inside her filled her with joy, but it was quickly overshadowed by worry and confusion. *How could this be possible? The only man I've been with is Henri, a vampire!*

Adele's thoughts were filled with anxiety as she tried to understand the changes in her body. She couldn't fathom how a pregnancy was possible, considering the father was a vampire. Henri had never mentioned anything about vampires being capable of reproducing.

Adele's mind raced with the impossibility of it all - vampires and humans couldn't possibly conceive of a child together; it defied the laws of nature. Yet, she couldn't deny the truth: she was sure she was pregnant with Henri's child. The reality of her situation was both astonishing and terrifying. How could this have happened? She couldn't understand the biology behind it, and the uncertainty was unsettling.

As she pondered what to do, Adele's mind raced with questions. Should she tell Henri about the pregnancy? Would he even care, or would he see it as an inconvenience? What if he didn't want to be involved? The thought of raising a child alone was terrifying.

Moreover, Adele was consumed by fear of Henri's reaction. Would he be enraged, disappointed, or perhaps even pleased? She couldn't even guess what Henri would say, nor would he even believe the child was his. And then, there was the question of their off-spring - what would it be like? Would the child inherit Henri's vampiric traits or be a normal human child? The possibilities swirled in her mind, each more unsettling than the last. A half-vampire child? The very thought sent shivers down her spine.

Adele knew she had to confront Henri, but discussing this with him made her uneasy. As the sun began to set, casting a golden glow over the deck, Adele steeled herself for the conversation that would change everything. With a deep breath, she made her way to the cabin, her heart heavy with concern for the future of her unborn child.

When she opened the cabin door, she noticed that the crew had cleaned the cabin, and the bodies were gone. She had been deep in thoughts on the deck that she had not realized they had done this. Thankfully, she sat on the bed, waiting for Henri to wake up. It would be soon, if at all, she mused. If Henri was tired from the killings, he might slumber all night and maybe the rest of the trip.

With a sigh, Adele acknowledged her growling stomach, remembering she had skipped lunch due to the morning's queasiness. Now, her hunger pangs were undeniable. She decided to head to the galley, seeking a nourishing meal and maybe calm her turbulent thoughts. Leaving the cabin behind, she walked across the hallway, and her nose followed the inviting aroma of food to the galley.

Men were sitting there. When they saw her, they gave her space by the table. Their wary glimpses showed that First Mate Rimini had told them what had happened.

"Good evening," she greeted them, glancing at the cook, who quickly brought her a bowl of soup and some slices of bread with a glass of red wine.

The tension and the silence in the galley made her scan the room. All the men were staring at her as if she was the monster. "Messieurs, I'm not the vampire. I work for him, just like you do now. He won't kill you if you do what he says." Her words seemed to calm the crew as they returned to their plates.

The cook asked, "What will happen when we reach the destination? Will he leave us alone and alive?"

"Yes, I believe so. He left me alive to help him through this trip across the ocean. He has no reason to drink your blood if he can stay in slumber the rest of the journey. I suggest that you keep quiet around the cabin so that he doesn't wake up hungry." Her eyes veered around the galley. "When we get to the destination harbor, I will take his coffin off this ship, and you are all free to do what you want." She continued eating with the men's eyes on her. However, her words assured them they wouldn't be killed like their comrades.

Chapter Forty-One

Adele And Henri

As Adele wandered the deck, she gazed wistfully at the fading sunbeams and the vibrant red and yellow hues of the horizon, worrying about what would happen in the cabin. She lingered, savoring the last views of the sun, yet her mind raced with anxiety. With a heavy sigh, she reluctantly returned to the cabin, her worries intensifying with each step, her thoughts worried about what Henri would say if he woke up.

She entered the cabin quietly, and after taking off her dress and shoes, she laid down on the bed, burying her face into the pillows, and started sobbing.

At the cabin, Henri was in deep slumber after the hectic journey during the storm and all the blood he had sustained from the crewmen. He had no intention of waking up. However, something bothered him. He thought he heard a quiet but consistent sound in the cabin. What was that noise? It bothered him so much that he opened his eyes in the coffin and pushed the lid aside.

His gaze swept the room, and his eyes landed on Adele lying in the bed, her body shaking with sobs. The sound he had heard was her weeping, a heart-wrenching cry that pierced his soul. He was taken aback, having never seen her like this before. Adele had always shown strength and resilience. This was so unlike her. Now, she seemed to crumble before his eyes, her tears revealing a pain he had never suspected she would carry. What could have caused such unbearable sorrow? Henri wondered and moved silently close to the bed. Her cry sounded like her heart was broken.

He sat down beside her, his weight on the bed causing the mattress to creak, and gently placed his hand on her shoulder, startling her so abruptly that she nearly leaped out of bed.

Adele's eyes widened in terror as she jerked away, her heart racing with the realization that she had unintentionally roused Henri from his slumber. Her face contorted in distress; she frantically wondered how to explain her tears and concerns to him.

Henri had always seen her strong side and how she had always confronted life's challenges with courage, like the time when he had left her in the alley bitten and alone. The woman he had gotten to know had never felt sorry for herself. She had always looked forward to facing challenges and trying to find a solution to her problems.

"Ah, Adele, what's amiss?" Henri asked, his voice laced with concern and tenderness as he continued to pat her back in a soothing motion. "Did one of the sailors offend you? Or perhaps something else has troubled you?" His words were soft and gentle, but his eyes searched hers with a deep longing to understand the source of her distress, his touch offering protection.

"No, they helped to take out the bodies, and they didn't complain or try to attack me," Adele said with a muffled voice. She turned her gaze to Henri, who saw her tear-striped cheeks and noted her eyes and nose were red. Sniffing, she added, "I was just overwhelmed with everything. I'm fine now." She lowered her gaze, knowing that she was lying.

Henri noticed how she turned away and did not reply to him. "You don't look fine. What's wrong?" Henri asked again in a tender voice.

"I'm pregnant!" Adele said almost inaudibly.

Henri sat there like a statue, not moving. His hand stopped patting Adele's back. After a long pause, he said, "That's impossible. It can't be my child."

"And yet I'm pregnant. I was a virgin when we met" Adele's eyes were now furious.

"That's what I mean. You can't be pregnant. It's been only two weeks."

"Your child is not like a normal human child. I can feel the baby moving inside me," Adele replied fiercely. "This one grows faster and is stronger."

"Vampires can't have children. They are undead," Henri protested.

"Are you certain?" Adele stared at him.

Henri had to admit he didn't know that much about vampires. That's why he wanted to find his creator to learn more about the undead and what it was like to live for centuries. "I don't know much about vampires."

"And I don't know much about having a child. We'll have to find help when we reach our destination," Adele replied.

Henri's mind raced with disbelief and uncertainty. *Pregnant? How could this be? Vampires didn't bear children. It was impossible.* And yet, Adele's words hung in the air like a challenge, a defiance of the very laws of nature that governed his immortal kind. He thought of their passion, their union... could it have somehow overcome the boundaries of their cursed existence? The prospect sent his thoughts reeling. *A child? Our child?* The idea was both exhilarating and terrifying. *What will this mean for our future? For our relationship, as she's a human and I'm a vampire?* Henri felt lost, torn between the joy of possibility and the dread of the unknown. *Could I truly be a father? And what will become of us all if this miracle is true?*

Henri's mind was filled with questions and doubts, but Adele's gaze held a quiet conviction, a determination that pierced his uncertainty. He took her hand, his touch gentle, seeking connection and understanding.

Henri's mind raced with the implications. They needed guidance, wisdom, and support. One name echoed in his mind—Joliette, his creator, and her coven. Yet, uncertainty shrouded their fate. Had their voyage ended well, or had the unforgiving sea claimed their ship, sending it to a watery grave with their coffins? Henri hoped they had reached their destination.

He wasn't sure where to look for Joliette either. She had only mentioned southern states. Joliette's coven had long coveted the grandest of estates, their wealth and opulence amassed over centuries of immortal life. But the French Revolution's bloody tide forced them to flee, seeking refuge from the guillotine's deadly blade and the sun's fiery wrath—either one would have killed them for sure.

Henri recalled that Joliette's dream was to establish a new coven, free from the darkness of the catacombs, where they could live in splendor and extravagance.

With her aristocratic background, she craved the finer things in life, and her vast wealth would indulge her every whim. Henri knew that her nocturnal nature might raise suspicions, but it could be dismissed as a quirky eccentricity, a charming habit of a foreign noble.

Yet, Henri was uncertain of Joliette's exact whereabouts, and locating her coven would be an overwhelming task, potentially taking weeks or even months.

This ship they were aboard was bound for Boston Harbor, a bustling hub for commercial traffic. They would start their next course there. Henri couldn't shake the uncertainty of whether Joliette had arrived at a different port. Only time would reveal the truth, he mused.

He also pondered if he would meet other vampires who could tell him more about the child born by a human. There had to be more vampires than just Joliette's coven, someone must know. But the trip was not over, and when they reached the harbor, they would need a carriage to travel further across a dangerous and new country. And now he had more than just himself to take care of.

Protecting Adele and their unborn child would be his most important task. He had never thought of having a child after being imprisoned in the Bastille and then choosing the life of the undead. He lifted his gaze, facing Adele. "We will figure this out. I will protect you and the child."

Chapter Forty-Two

The Last Days Before Boston

As the days went by slowly and inevitably, the ship neared her destination, Boston. Gone were the strong stormy winds and turbulent waters. Now, her white sails billowed in the gentle caress of the wind. The rhythmic lapping of the waves against the hull created a soothing melody in the otherwise gloomy journey.

One by one, the sailors fell prey to the mysterious forces that lurked in the shadows, their necks bearing the telltale signs of bruises and fang marks. Adele, no longer concerned with concealing her bruised neck, moved in and out of her cabin swiftly and quietly, her eyes cast downward to avoid the accusatory gazes of the crewmen.

Mealtimes in the galley were somber affairs, the silence punctuated only by the clinking of utensils against tin plates. Adele hastened through her meals, her eyes fixed on the plate. She could feel the sailors' gloomy stares on her, and the atmosphere was heavy with silent accusations. She retreated to the solitude of her cabin, her footsteps quiet on the creaking wooden floorboards, lest she disturb the slumbering Henri in his coffin.

On the last day of the trip, the strong winds returned. The ship creaked and groaned, its wooden hull straining against the relentless push of the waves as if echoing the turmoil that brewed within its passengers. The winds howled and whipped through the sails, their mournful sighs weaving a haunting refrain that seemed to whisper secrets to the waves below.

Every night was similar: Henri made love to Adele with passion and urgency, and the crew members suffered from his insatiable hunger for blood. However, there weren't many hours left to reach the destination...

As the morning sun colored the horizon, Tempest Lady docked in Boston Harbor, and Adele stood on the deck, her long hair cascading down on her back, gazing out at the bustling port. The first sun rays cast a golden glow over the crowded docks and warehouses. Adele felt a mix of emotions: relief at finally reaching their destination, anxiety about what lay ahead, and a deep concern for the future of her unborn child. She tried to push away the uneasiness from her thoughts as she suspected Henri could sense it in his coffin.

As the crewmen hastened to transport the coffin from the ship to the harbor, their eagerness to bid farewell to the mysterious cargo was palpable. Adele, with a gentle smile, extended a small pouch to the first mate. "Please accept this token of our gratitude. Henri wished to express his appreciation for your kindness and assistance during our journey."

The first mate's eyes widened in surprise as he opened the pouch, revealing a dozen glittering gold coins within. "Thank you, ma'am," he said, his voice filled with gratitude. "May fortune favor you and yours." With a respectful bow, he swiftly departed, leaving Adele alone on the bustling docks, the coffin beside her.

Adele's hand reached out, her fingers tracing the wooden lid with a gentle touch. "We've arrived, Henri," she whispered, her voice barely audible over the commotion of the harbor. "We've reached the shores of Boston. Our journey has finally come to an end." Once a symbol of confinement, the coffin now represented a new beginning, a threshold to the unknown.

Now, she would have to find a harbor master or someone to help her with the coffin and find a safe place to stay until night. The harbor master's office was nearby, and Adele found an elderly gentleman sitting there browsing some notes. When she entered, he glimpsed her. "Good morning, ma'am. I believe you arrived this morning on Tempest Lady. That ship was late from her schedule."

"Yes, she was. However, I'm here now with my dear father's coffin, and I need transportation." Adele looked stern.

"Of course, ma'am. Where are you heading, if I may ask?"

"My father had distant relatives in southern states, so we had planned to go find them before his demise." Adele kept her gaze toward the floor, looking timid and sad.

"Ah, my condolences, ma'am," the harbor master said, his voice filled with sympathy. "Let me assist you with the carriage, and my men will help with the c-offin." He beckoned to a young boy, who scurried over to help with the tasks. "Here, lad, help the lady with her carriage, and then we'll settle the gentlemen's coffin ."

The boy nodded eagerly, his eyes wide with curiosity, as he began to help Adele with the carriage while the harbor master directed the men to carefully lift the coffin and follow behind. Soon, Adele sat in the driver's seat of her new carriage, which she had paid for, heading south.

Chapter Forty-Three

Henri Awakens

Night had fallen over the bustling harbor, the only sound being the distant sounds of the waves against the shoreline and the sounds of the city.

Adele had stopped her carriage in an alley on the outskirts of the harbor and decided to wait there. Wearing her black dress, she was barely visible in the darkness. She sat beside the coffin, keeping her eyes on the lid, waiting for the moment she knew would come. Suddenly, the coffin creaked open, and Henri emerged, his eyes gleaming in the moonlight.

He stretched his lean frame, his movements graceful and fluid as he took in their surroundings. The harbor was quiet, the only signs of life coming from the distant taverns and the occasional passing of a night watchman.

Henri's gaze settled on Adele, and he smiled, his fangs glinting in the moonlight. "My dear, we have arrived," he said, his voice low and husky. "But our journey is far from over."

He turned to survey their surroundings, his eyes scanning the dark alleys and narrow streets that led into the heart of Boston. "We need to find Joliette's coven," he muttered to himself. "She said she would leave a note to a harbormaster's office or in a tavern at the harbor."

"The harbormaster didn't say anything when I acquired a carriage. I don't believe he knew anything." Adele stood up, her eyes fixed on Henri's profile.

"Where will we go?" she asked, her voice barely above a whisper.

Henri's gaze settled on a nearby tavern, its sign creaking in the gentle breeze. "We will start there," he said, his eyes glinting with a hint of mischief. "Rumors and information flow like ale in such places. We will gather our bearings and plan our next move." He tapped his vest's pocket where Joliette's piece of paper was. That was the address she had given him. However, he had no idea if her plans had changed after that or if they even had reached Boston Harbor.

Henri knew that after their grueling sea voyage, the vampires would be parched and fatigued, their bodies craving the rejuvenating elixir of blood. It was only logical that they would seek to satiate their thirst and replenish their strength as soon as possible. Someone unfortunate enough to cross their path would have fallen prey to their hunger, leaving behind a trail of clues for Henri to follow.

"Wait here, I will be back soon." Without another word, he strode towards the tavern. Adele stayed behind, her heart pounding with excitement and a hint of fear. She sat in the carriage, hoping that no one came to check up on it and wishing that the night watchman would hasten his steps and come by soon... The harbor was not the best place for a young lady to be alone, and this was a strange new country. However, she found solace in the thought that Henri's keen hearing would notice her scream for help if something happened.

Chapter Forty-Four

Henri In The Tavern

The tavern, nestled in the heart of Boston Harbor, was a rustic, weathered building that seemed to lean toward the road. The wooden sign creaked in the gentle breeze, bearing the words "The Hefty Tavern" in faded red letters with the added information: "food & spirits" below it. The door, adorned with a brass doorknob shaped like an anchor, swung open with a creak.

As Henri entered the tavern, his keen eyes darted around, noticing the sailors on the tables and in the bar.

Inside, the air was thick with the smell of ale and smoke. The walls, adorned with fishing nets and nautical trinkets, seemed to whisper tales of the brave sailors in their boats. The wooden bar, polished to a sheen, stretched like a welcoming arm, inviting patrons to come.

Flickering candles and lanterns cast a warm, golden glow, illuminating the faces of the sailors, their laughter and chatter mingling with the clinking of glasses and the occasional burst of laughter.

Behind the bar, a stout man with a bushy beard and a twinkle in his eye poured ale and whiskey with a generous hand, his laughter booming like a sea captain's as he regaled the patrons with tales of the past.

Leisurely, Henri strolled toward the counter and ordered a glass of wine. Lifting his eyebrows, the bartender fulfilled his order, even though it wasn't normal in this establishment. He had already assessed the guest was a gentleman and a foreigner based on his accent and outfit. After paying for the drink, he sipped it and then met the bartender's gaze again. "Very good wine you have here, my friend."

"Thank you, sir. That's very kind of you to say." The bartender chuckled and nodded in appreciation. "Ah, glad you're enjoying it, sir! That's a special vintage, imported from the finest wineries in Europe. We don't get many folks coming in here who can appreciate a good wine, so it's a pleasure to see you savoring' it." He wiped his meaty hand on his apron and leaned in, his voice takin' on a conspiratorial tone. "If you're looking' for something even more...exotic, I might have something in the back that'll suit your taste." He raised an eyebrow, inviting Henri to take a ch ance.

Shaking his head, Henri replied, "I'm looking for some of my friends. I had hoped they had left me a word here," Henri started. "It was a group of ten, I believe. They left France earlier than I did. They had not left any letter in the harbor master's office, and that's why I'm checking here," Henri explained.

"Do you know the ship they arrived in? What did they look like?" the bartender wiped the counter with a cloth. He already guessed who the man meant, but he wanted to be sure before divulging the information to a stranger.

"The ship was called Sainte Basile," Henri said and added, "The woman I'm looking at was a beautiful young woman with dark hair, and she was accompanied by an elderly man wearing a fancy suit, an elderly grey-haired woman, and a young woman. I don't know exactly how many left Paris with them. They all fled the chaos in the city after the revolution. I only know a few of them," Henri admitted. He hadn't paid attention to all the coven members, and now he could recall only Joliette, Armand, Benedicta, and Minette.

"I believe I met them about eight weeks ago," the bartender's voice was casual, but his expression turned wary. He stopped wiping the counter, his hand hovering in mid-air, and his eyes narrowed as he met Henri's gaze. The bartender's eyes seemed to bore into Henri's as if searching for something hidden beneath the surface. "What's your business with them, sir? he asked, his voice low and cautious.

"They were supposed to leave me a message where to buy a house." Henri's reply was casual.

"After their ship arrived, we had a string of attacks in the harbor area. I'm not saying the passengers were responsible, but... well, the rumors spread around here, whispers of a demon on their ship, bringing darkness and terror to our shores."

Henri knew now that this was the right place. The bartender had met Joliette and the others. Their ship had passed the ocean, and they had not sunk into its cold embrace.

The bartender leaned to pick up a note under the counter. "The lady with the raven black hair left this note. She said to give it to a young man who will come looking for her. She knew you would come."

Henri accepted the note from the bartender's hand, his fingers brushing against the rough skin. He then placed a gold coin on the counter, the metal clinking against the wood. "She trusts me," he said, his voice low and mysterious, before turning to leave.

But the bartender's voice stopped him, a low, gravelly warning: "Don't stay around here too long, sir. Anything can happen." The words sent a shiver down Henri's spine, but he didn't look back. Instead, he lifted his hand in a brief greeting and strode briskly out of the tavern, the door creaking shut behind him.

As he emerged into the cool night air, Henri quickened his pace, his long legs carrying him swiftly toward the waiting carriage. The bartender's warning lingered in his mind, and a sense of unease that he couldn't shake.

Chapter Forty-Five

Henri and Adele Flee
from the Harbor

"Did you find out anything?" Adele asked when Henri appeared from the darkness and opened the carriage door.

"Yes, Joliette had left a note for me there, but I think we might be in grave danger here. We better leave before the sailors come after us," Henri said, closing the carriage door again. Quickly, he climbed onto the driver's seat and urged the horses to run.

The night sky was inky black, as the clouds covered the sky. It started raining. First, just a little bit of drizzle, and then it turned into pouring rain. Henri thanked God because he knew that not many people would be out in that weather, and their escape from the harbor would be easier.

The only sound was the soft clip-clop of the horses' hooves on the cobblestone streets, echoing off the buildings. Henri sat tall and alert, his eyes fixed on the road ahead as he guided the carriage through the silent streets of Boston.

The gas lamps lining the streets danced with flickering flames, casting eerie shadows on the pavement. The air was thick with the damp, loamy scent of moist earth and the acrid tang of smoke from the torches and lamps. Amidst these familiar aromas, Henri's nostrils caught the tantalizing whiffs of sizzling meat and boiling potatoes, wafting from nearby homes.

As they made their way south, the streets grew increasingly deserted, the only signs of life coming from the screeches of night owls or the distant howl of a wolf. The carriage wheels creaked and groaned, the sound echoing through the still night.

Henri's eyes scanned the shadows, his senses on high alert, as though he expected the sailors to come after him from the tavern. He glanced over his shoulder, making sure that they were traveling alone and that no one was following. The horses seemed to sense his tension, their ears pricked and their eyes rolling nervously as they picked up on his unease.

Adele sat inside the carriage in silence, the darkness outside seeming to press in on her. She kept looking outside to see where they were heading.

The rain stopped, and the moon came out, lighting the empty road ahead.

Suddenly, a figure emerged from the shadows, his face obscured by a mask and a wide-brimmed hat. He brandished a pistol, its barrel glinting in the faint moonlight.

Adele gasped, her hand flying to her mouth in terror.

"Stand and deliver!" he barked, his voice gruff and menacing.

Pulling the horses' reins, Henri stopped. "Leave us be. You don't want to bother us," Henri yelled back. Henri's eyes narrowed, waiting for the robber's reaction. He knew he could kill him immediately, but he would waste more nighttime and, thus, also the travel time, if he had to take care of this stupid man who didn't know who he was dealing with.

The robber took a step closer, his pistol trained on Henri's chest. "I said, stand and deliver!"

Without hesitation, Henri leaped from the carriage, his canines flashing in the moonlight. The robber's eyes widened in surprise, but he didn't back down.

The two men clashed. Henri grabbed the man's gun, throwing it aside and then sinking his teeth into his neck with deadly precision.

The man's eyes went wide with shock. He crumpled to the ground, and Henri drank his blood.

Henri stood up, his chest heaving with ragged breaths, his body still trembling with the aftermath of the rapid transformation. The primal force of vampirism that lurked just beneath his surface had been satiated, but the cost was evident in the tension that still coursed through his veins. As he regained control, his breathing slowed, and his muscles relaxed, releasing the coiled energy that had fueled his transformation. His gaze cleared, and he looked down at his hands, now steady and still, as if marveling at the contrast between his tranquil appearance and the recent turbulent forces within him.

Henri's thoughts were a jumble of emotions – relief, guilt, and a deep-seated fear and respect of the immortal being he had become. He knew he had found a way to control this hungry demon but did not know how to tame the thirst that threatened to consume him whole. He feared losing himself forever to its primal power.

Adele's voice was barely audible, her words a whispered prayer of thanks.

The horses whinnied nervously, their eyes rolling white with fear. Henri climbed back into the carriage, his eyes scanning the darkness for any further threats.

As they drove away, the robber's body grew smaller in the distance, Adele sighed in relief. She was safe with Henri.

Chapter Forty-Six

The Long Night

The night air was cool and crisp. Henri cracked the reins, urging the horses on as the carriage rumbled through the night. He wanted to get past the tree-lined road to more open space as he didn't want to be stopped again by some road bandit while Adele had to deal with it.

Adele sat inside the carriage, her eyes fixed on the road ahead, her face pale and drawn. She was exhausted, but she knew they couldn't stop yet. Not until the first light of dawn crept over the horizon.

As the hours passed, the darkness seemed to grow shorter. Henri's eyes burned with fatigue, but he refused to yield. He had to keep driving, had to put as much distance between them so that it would be safe to stop, and he could go to rest in his coffin. The further from the city harbor they got, the better. There wouldn't be any rumors of foreigners being the devils. Unless Joliette's coven had continued to ravage the countryside while moving forward to their new destination.

Finally, after what felt like an eternity, the sky began to lighten. The first rays of sunshine crept over the horizon, casting a golden glow over the landscape. Henri's heart sank, knowing he had to stop. Henri's strength began to wane. He could feel the weight of his vampiric curse bearing down on him, the need for rest and darkness growing more urgent by the minute. He stopped the carriage and climbed down.

"Adele," he said, his voice low and husky, "take the reins. I must rest."

Adele nodded, her eyes wide with understanding.

As Henri opened the coffin, a wave of relief washed over him as he settled in it. He sank into the darkness, the softness of the velvet-lined box enveloping him like a shroud.

"Keep driving, Adele," Henri whispered, his voice barely audible. "Keep driving until nightfall. I'll rest now, but I'll be back, stronger and more determined than ever."

Adele's eyes were fixed on Henri's pale face as he settled into the coffin. She knew the drill all too well, as she had seen it countless times before. The sun's rays were poison to Henri's kind, and he needed the darkness to rejuvenate.

Henri pulled the lid close.

After witnessing this, Adele stepped out of the carriage and climbed onto the driver's seat, taking the reins in her hands once more. The horses whinnied softly, sensing a new driver, but she soothed them with a gentle voice and a pat on the neck.

As the sun rose higher in the sky, Adele urged the horses on, their pace steady and relentless. She didn't know where this road was going, but she knew that the further they got, the better chances she had of having her baby.

The hours ticked by, the sun beating down on her like a hammer. Adele's skin prickled with sweat, her eyes scanning the horizon for any sign of trouble. She knew they couldn't stop until nightfall, when Henri would emerge from his coffin, refreshed and ready to take the reins once more.

The landscape blurred around her, a never-ending stretch of trees and hills, as she drove on, her heart heavy with the weight of their journey. She didn't know what lay ahead, but she knew one thing for certain: with Henri by her side, she could face anything the treacherous new world threw their way. Her thoughts went to Joliette. What would she say when she learned Henri had impregnated her? Would she be angry or jealous? Adele had no idea if Joliette had any feelings toward Henri except that he was part of her coven and that she was his creator.

Chapter Forty-Seven

The Baudelaire Brothers

"**W**here is Charles? He should have been back by now," Grant, the eldest Baudelaire brother, muttered, his eyes fixed on the intricately crafted clock in the corner of the grand dining room. Its ticking was loud, a reminder of the passing hours. The room itself was a masterclass in opulence, with gilded red wallpaper that shimmered like rubies in the flickering candlelight. Mahogany furniture, polished to a high sheen, seemed to glow with golden candlelight. The delicate porcelain dishes adorned the table. Their painted floral patterns danced across the plates' surface like a fairytale garden.

The chandelier with candles hung above the table was a dazzling array of crystal and silver, refracting the light into a kaleidoscope of colors.

The air was heavy with the scent of cooked meat and the faint aroma of cigar smoke, hinting at the family's taste for meat. And yet, despite the luxurious surroundings, a sense of unease hung in the air, like the whispered warning of a coming storm. "He should give up this thieving of passing carriages," Albert, the second brother, added, his voice laced with concern. "He thinks it's fun and exciting, but what if one day he meets someone who is not afraid of him?"

The clock ticked on, its rhythmic beat a reminder that time was running out, and the darkness that lurked beyond the edges of their gilded world was waiting to pounce.

"I won't wait any longer." Grant pushed his chair away from the table. "I'll go look for him. What if something has happened to him."

"I'll join you." Albert followed his brother outside to the stables, where they got their horses.

They galloped towards the forest, heading toward the road passing through it. This was Charles' hunting ground, where he lay in wait for the unsuspecting travelers who ventured there. His preferred ambush spot was a bend in the road, a treacherous curve where the trees seemed to close in on the path. It was a spot carefully chosen for its concealment, where the approaching carriages were blinded by the twist in the road until it was too late. Charles would be hiding in the shadows, his eyes fixed on the road, his senses primed for the perfect moment to strike.

The trees seemed to whisper secrets to each other as the Baudelaire brothers rode closer, their leaves rustling ominously in the wind. Their keen sense of smell caught a strange scent before they saw the slaughtered body on the roadside. The corpse was a mangled mess, ravaged by the nocturnal scavengers that roamed the forest. Charles' fingers were nowhere to be found, torn from his hands like branches from a tree. His cheek was a bloody crater, a chunk of flesh gouged out by some ravenous beast. The body was a grim view, a reminder that even the mighty Baudelaires were not immune. The scent of death and decay hung heavy in the air, a morbid perfume that clung to the dead brother like a shroud.

"Charles!" Grant jumped off the road, rushing to his brother's side only to caress his dead body in his arms. "Who did this to you, brother?" he whispered, his voice filled with sadness.

Albert kneeled next to him, studying the wounds. "This was no ordinary traveler." He gestured to the wounds. "He has two puncture marks on his neck, and his skin is white, too white for his age. And look at the other wounds: no blood. Someone took his blood and left the corpse behind." His voice was calculated, and his eyes flashed with anger. "I've heard of this kind of a creature: they came to this land from across the sea. I bet this one arrived in one of the tall ships and filled his need for blood by killing our poor Charles."

Grant stood up, cradling Charles's body in his arms. "We are the Baudelaires. I swear we will revenge this. Whoever did this can't be far away. Charles, we will find your killer and take his life or the life of his loved one." The ominous threat echoed in the early morning forest. The forest fell silent. They knew who these brothers were. They took the body back into their mansion and then went after the killers.

The Baudelaires were a ruthless and ancient clan that had terrorized the East Coast for generations. Their wealth and power were matched only by their sinister secret: they were shape-shifters, werewolves, cursed to unleash their inner beasts beneath the full moon's glow. The nearby villages lived in perpetual dread, barricading themselves indoors as the lunar cycle reached its peak, praying that the Baudelaires' bloodlust would not come knocking on their doors. And now, with one of their own lying dead, the family's wrath would surely be unleashed, casting a shadow of terror over the land.

Chapter Forty-Eight

The Pursuit

A dele's hands gripped the reins tightly as she navigated the carriage through the forest, the early morning sunlight casting a golden glow over the trees. Henri's coffin rested securely in the back, his peaceful slumber a stark contrast to the beautiful morning. Adele felt a growing unease. She didn't know why.

After two hours of carriage ride, Adele's anxiety spiraled out of control, her heart racing like a wild animal trapped in her chest. She kept glancing over her shoulder, trying to assure herself that everything was fine. The empty road behind the carriage only seemed to mock her. The silence was oppressive, heavy with the weight of unspoken threats. Her mind raced with worst-case scenarios, each one more terrifying than the last. The memory of the bandit's lifeless body and Henri's deadly efficiency did little to calm her fears.

Adele's breath came in short gasps, her senses on high alert as if anticipating something evil to happen. The world around her seemed to be holding its breath, waiting for the other shoe to drop, and Adele's very soul trembled with fear.

The air was crisp and cool, filled with the sweet scent of blooming wildflowers. But Adele's tranquility was short-lived, as the sound of galloping hooves echoed through the forest, growing louder with each passing moment. She glanced over her shoulder, her

heart sinking as she saw two horsemen closing in on her
.

The two riders hurtled toward her with a fierce intensity, leaving no doubt that they were hell-bent on capturing her. The realization struck Adele, sending an icy terror coursing through her veins. Her heart raced as she grasped the gravity of her situation, her mind reeling with the ominous implications.

The riders' thundering approach seemed to grow louder, their horses' pounding hooves echoing through the forest like a death sentence, leaving her with a sense of desperation and impending doom...

Adele knew she couldn't urge the horses any faster, their exhausted bodies laboring after a long night, their breathless panting a stark reminder of the limitations of their strength.

The brothers' relentless approach seemed to mock her, their horses' pounding hooves echoing through the forest like a death knell, leaving her with a sense of hopelessness and impending doom.

"Mon Dieu," Adele whispered, her voice trembling.

The brothers drew closer, their eyes fixed on the carriage with an unnerving intensity. Adele cracked the reins, trying to urge the horses to go faster, but to no avail.

The Baudelaires were gaining ground. Their faces were a few feet from the carriage now, their breath visible in the chill morning air.

Adele's gaze fell upon the Baudelaire brothers, and her heart sank. Their faces were twisted in a fury so palpable that it seemed to radiate from them like a dark aura. Her mind raced, trying to figure out what to do. She knew without any conversation that the brothers' ire was directed at her and Henri. The memory of the bandit's lifeless body, left in their wake, flashed before her eyes. She slowed down as she realized she and Henri were now at the mercy of these fierce and unforgiving-looking men.

"Stop the carriage!" the eldest brother bellowed, his voice like a crack of thunder.

Adele's heart raced as she realized she couldn't outrun them. With a deep, shuddering breath, she gave up the flight and pulled the reins hard, bringing the carriage to a halt. The Baudelaires rode next to her, their eyes blazing with a feral intensity in the morning light. "What do you want?" Adele asked, lifting her chin, looking bravely directly into the eyes of the first rider. She could smell the man. His scent was feral, animal-like, and his eyes were predator's eyes.

"My brother Charles Baudelaire was left to die on the roadside. I want to know if you were involved in his death," the first rider asked, holding his black stallion so close Adele could feel the horse's breath on her.

Adele sniffed and swallowed hard. "He attacked us." Her voice was soft, fragile.

"And you killed him," the other rider sneered, his voice dripping with malice. "Now it's your turn."

Chapter Forty-Nine

Adele and the Brothers

Adele felt terror like she had never felt before. *These two men think I killed the bandit! They don't know about Henri...*

She kept her eyes on the older brother and asked, "Why do you think it was me, sir?"

"Because your carriage is the only one on this road. We know where our brother usually preyed on the carriages. His body was in one of his favorite spots."

The man's face turned purple, and he spat on the ground. "He was left there like trash on the roadside! My brother!" His voice dripped with malice when he said the last words.

Grant pulled Adele down from the seat, and she fell to the ground.

Albert opened the carriage and peeked inside. "There's no one else here. Just the coffin. It had to be her. She's the beast!" In his anger, he dragged the coffin and pushed it off the carriage and to the roadside. When he kicked it on its side, the lid fell open. Henri's still body tumbled partly out of the coffin. Luckily, the shade of the trees and part of the lid covered his body. Otherwise, he would have suffered a painful death in the sunlight. He had listened to the argument, but he couldn't do anything to help Adele. It was daytime. He would be dead before he even reached either one of the attackers.

Adele's eyes followed the coffin, and he stifled a cry. Placing her hand over her mouth, she feared what would happen next to her and her unborn child.

Grant's eyes transformed into wolf-like yellow orbs, his teeth sharpening into razor-sharp fangs. "You took one from our family. I will take your life." He leaned closer and bit her into her shoulder, pulling her tender white skin with her teeth.

Screaming in terror, Adele tried to move away. Her desperate plea tore through the air: "Please, I'm pregnant. Save my child!"

For an instant, Grant's eyes widened in shock, his gaze froze on Adele's trembling form. Then, his face contorted in a cruel laugh, his head thrown back in sadistic glee. "Ah, even better!" he exclaimed, his voice dripping with malice. "We'll raise the child as one of our own, a true beast born of blood and darkness!"

He leaned closer and ripped Adele's clothes apart, revealing her stomach. He showed her his long taupe-colored nails, sharp as daggers. He placed his forefinger's nail on top of her belly and pushed it inside and pulled the skin open with a sharp downward motion.

Adele's scream echoed in the forest. It was a sound that chilled to the bone.

Grant pulled out the child and handed it to Albert. He stared at Adele on the ground. "The forest animals will soon find you because of the fresh blood smell... unless you bleed to death before that."

As the brothers rode away, leaving Adele to her fate, she whispered to Henri, "Mon amour, please... save our child if you survive."

Henri's muffled voice vowed, "Adele, I will. I swear." But the horror of their situation was far from over. He wondered how the child would even survive without her mother. Adele's pregnancy was far from full term, yet her child grew at an alarming rate, defying the norms of human development. Unbeknownst to Henri, the werewolf's tainted saliva had infected Adele's bloodstream, passing on its dark legacy to their unborn child. The fetus now carried the essence of three species: human, vampire, and werewolf. This unholy trinity would shape the child's destiny, making her a singular being unlike any other in existence.

Adele's world became unimaginably cold, and darkness consumed her, her body succumbing to the unimaginable trauma.

Meanwhile, Henri fought against the excruciating pain of the sunlight, his skin burning with every inch exposed. He managed to drag himself back into the shadows, his body screaming in agony.

As the sun continued its relentless assault, Henri's vision began to blur, his strength waning. He knew he had to hold on for Adele's sake and that of their child. With a Herculean effort, he pulled himself back into the coffin, the lid closing over him like a shield.

In the darkness, Henri's thoughts raced with a mix of rage, fear, and determination. He vowed to survive, to protect their child from the monsters that had slaughtered Adele. The silence was oppressive; the only sound was the breathing of the forest animals, waiting to claim Adele's lifeless body.

Time ticked by, each passing moment a struggle for Henri's survival. The sun's grip on the forest slowly loosened, and the shadows grew longer, beckoning the night to come and bring with it a chance for Henri to rise and fight back.

Chapter Fifty

The Chase

As the sun dipped below the horizon, the forest succumbed to the darkness, and Henri's strength began to revive. He emerged from the coffin, his eyes scanning the surroundings with rage and determination. The memory of Adele's screams and the brutality of the two men fueled his steps.

He saw Adele's body on the ground. The wound on her stomach looked gruesome. So much dried blood everywhere. The blood made his senses alert. He sniffed her body and smelled a strange, animal-like scent. The man who assaulted her had left a trail of scent behind. He took Adele's body and carried it to the forest. He laid her body on a grass bed and said a silent prayer. "Adele, my love, I don't know if God listens to us vampires, but I hope he will take your soul to heaven. You were never evil. I was your ruin. When you met me, you were doomed. Sleep peacefully in your eternal rest." He knew that the animals would come and rip her apart, so he carried heavy stones over her body and buried her under them. He knew he had lost a lot of time doing that, but he couldn't leave Adele's body behind.

When he returned to the road, the carriage was there. The horses were tired, so Henri let them lose and go. He would travel faster as a bat. With a swift and silent movement, Henri pursued the werewolves, his vampire senses guiding him through the forest. The moon cast an eerie glow, illuminating the path ahead. Henri's decision was made: he would rescue his child and exact vengeance on the monsters that had destroyed his life.

The wind rushed past him as he flew, and his wings barely moved as he glided through the sky. The distance between him and the werewolves narrowed, their scent growing stronger with every flap of the wings. Henri's eyes blazed with a fierce light, his fangs bared in a snarl.

The question echoed in his mind: would he catch them before they reached their mansion, or would they escape, taking his child forever? The chase was on, and only the night would tell. What was the name he heard they mentioned? *Charles Baudelaire. He was the bandit. The two other men were his brothers...*

He slowed down. Several large mansions were ahead and also villages. He could smell the scent of the men, and it was getting stronger. However, now he wondered if it was wise to go after them without a plan. The smell of the brothers was strong and feral. It was not a normal human smell. It made him hesitate. The way they had treated Adele was not usual either.

Instead of going after the smell, he landed on the rooftop of the nearby village and transformed back into a human before entering a pub. The bartender was friendly enough and advised where he could find a new horse and where to rest after a long journey.

"Are you going to stay in this area for a while, sir?" the bartender inquired.

"I think I will rest here for a day and then continue my journey tomorrow," Henri suggested

The bartender glanced at him. "It would be better to stay overnight. Tomorrow is the full moon. It's not safe to travel during the moonlight."

Henri asked, "Why?"

"The Baudelaires," the bartender replied. "They are werewolves. They will rip you apart if they find you moving outside."

That was the strange smell, Henri thought as he finished his drink and thanked the bartender. He walked to the inn the bartender had recommended.

As Henri stepped into the rustic inn, the scent of wood smoke and worn leather enveloped him. The elderly innkeeper, polishing a mug with a worn towel, looked up with a mix of curiosity and caution. Henri's gaze locked onto the man, his eyes weary from the long journey. "Sir, I require assistance. My carriage lies broken on the road, and I need a new one – or a horse – to press on." He paused, his voice low and urgent. "Time is not on my side."

The innkeeper's bushy eyebrows rose. "Boston, you say? That's a long haul. What brings you out here, alone and in such haste?"

Henri's smile was fleeting. "Family obligations. I must reach them before... complications arise." The innkeeper's eyes sparkled with intrigue, but Henri offered no further explanation. Instead, he said, "I'd like to have a room to stay for a day and then I will continue to my destination."

"I have a room available," the innkeeper said, his tone measured. "But be warned, traveling by night is treacherous. You'd do well to wait till the following morning."

Henri's gaze was firm. "I appreciate your concern, but I must go on. I will only sleep a day and then return to the road. My family awaits." The word "family" hung in the air, heavy with unspoken meaning. Henri had not exactly lied as he considered his coven as his new family.

With arrangements made, Henri ascended to his room, drawing the curtains shut behind him. "Do not disturb me during the day," he instructed the innkeeper, his voice stern but polite.

He knew the carriage he had used was left on the road, but he hesitated to return there. He recalled hearing that one brother had always hunted along that road, so maybe it would be wiser not to take that road but find another one. But he didn't want to go there and be reminded of Adele's horrific death. He could still hear her screams of terror in his mind.

I'm stranded with only the clothes on my back and valuables in my pockets. The thought of returning to the scene of Adele's tragic fate crossed his mind, but he hesitated. *If the Baudelaires are indeed robbers, they likely returned to the crime scene and plundered our abandoned luggage, and, in doing so, discovered that there are clothes for both a man and a woman.* A chilling realization dawned on Henri – *They might be lying in wait for my return!* He decided it was too risky to go back.

He lay down on the bed and closed his eyes. His slow, deep breath was the only sound in the room.

What should I do? Should I go after my child or try to find Joliette?

We were in a hurry to leave Boston Harbor, and I did not even read the note I had received from the tavern. Sitting up, he searched his pocket, pulled out a folded note, and opened it.

Mon Cher Henri,

If you receive this note, you have found a way to cross the ocean, and I'm pleased to welcome you to the new continent. We will head toward a city called New Orleans. I have purchased several houses there. If you can, please join us there.

Je t'embrasse très fort,

Joliette

I'm only one vampire, Henri thought, *but with Joliette's support, I could save my child. I can't go against a clan of werewolves by myself. They are not normal humans. The wise thing would be to let things calm down. The Baudelaires have my child, but they didn't say they would kill her. When time passes, they will be less cautious, and it will be easier to penetrate their stronghold.* Flinching, his thoughts returned to the killing he had witnessed. *The killers didn't give Adele a chance. They didn't even consider who the child's father was*, Henri thought. His hands balled into a fist.

I promised Adele I would find our child and revenge her death. I will keep my promise. It won't help our child if I rush into a trap and get killed. No one would know about her after my death. I need to inform Joliette and the other coven members that she exists, Henri thought, and his decision was made.

My knowledge of werewolves is limited, but I do know they're shapeshifters. The Baudelaires, who roam this village and the surrounding forest, are a prime ex-

ample. But do their powers extend beyond the full moon, or are they confined to that one phase of the month? I need to gather more information about their kind before launching a daring raid on their lair. Joliette, with her vast knowledge, is my best bet for uncovering the secrets I seek.

Next, Henri's thoughts went on the journey ahead. *How do I get to New Orleans? I can rent a carriage, and I doubt I can find a new coffin. That means I can only travel at night. Perhaps I can sleep in taverns during my journey and then continue at dusk. It could work.*

At dawn, he drifted into a restless sleep.

Chapter Fifty-One

The Journey to New Orleans

Henri's eyes fluttered open as the sun dipped below the horizon. He rose from the bed, his mind refreshed and focused on the journey ahead. He requested a carriage and horses from the innkeeper, emphasizing the need for speed and discretion.

With a deep breath, Henri climbed to the driver's seat, grasped the reins, and urged the horses forward, the carriage wheels creaking into motion. His expression grim, he steadied himself to the perilous journey ahead. New Orleans, with Joliette and her coven, beckoned him, the only destination where he might find solace and a glimmer of hope. The horses' hooves echoed through the silent streets as they departed, leaving the village and its dark memories behind.

As Henri journeyed south, the days merged into a haze of slumber in taverns and roadside inns in darkened rooms. And his nocturnal travel was lonely – the only sounds accompanying him were the creaks and groans of the carriage and the steady beat of the horses' hooves.

The relentless thirst for blood drove him to experiment with nocturnal forest creatures, but their blood proved unsatisfying, failing to sustain him for long. Thus, he resorted to preying upon solitary travelers under the cover of darkness, taking only enough blood to sustain his journey, careful to leave his victims alive yet unwitting participants in his quest for survival.

At night, he'd continue his journey, the moon casting an eerie glow over the landscape. His thoughts oscillated between his child's fate and the looming encounter with Joliette. Could she help him with the werewolf clan and tell him more about their kind – what are their weaknesses and strengths? How could he possibly rescue his child from their clutches? And his child raised another burning question: how did he even have a child with Adele?

With each passing mile, Henri's resolve hardened, driven by the unyielding promise to rescue his child and avenge Adele's tragic fate. The memory of his beloved companion, brutally taken by the werewolves, seared his heart, kindling a fierce determination to seek Joliette for help. The flames of revenge burned bright, fueling his journey as he pressed onward. The blackness of the night matched the darkness in his soul as he raced toward the unknown, his heart consumed by a singular purpose: to save his child and exact retribution from the monsters that had destroyed his family.

New Orleans

New Orleans beckoned Henri, a city shrouded in mystery and magic where the living and the undead coexisted. After weeks of travel, the carriage finally approached the outskirts of New Orleans. It was early in the evening, and the sun had just set.

Henri's heart raced as he gazed upon the city's sprawling landscape, a tapestry of grand mansions, crumbling cottages, and winding streets.

His keen sense of smell picked up the floral scents in the air: magnolias, jasmine, and roses. He realized it was already late spring. The time went by fast when you had to run for your life, travel across the sea and then all the other things that happened. Henri had not even paid attention to seasonal changes around him. It felt like it was just yesterday when he was in the Bastille's cell waiting for his beheading.

As the carriage rattled over the cobblestones, Henri's eyes scanned the streets, taking in the vibrant markets, the ornate ironwork, and the residents – a melting pot of humans and other creatures. As he went by, he was sure he recognized a group of vampires lounging in the shade, their eyes gleaming like diamonds in the moonlight.

Should I ask them where I can find Joliette? He pondered, but his impatience got the better of him. He opted to stable his carriage and horses and embark on a quest to find her himself.

With a sense of determination, he stepped out into the vibrant streets of New Orleans, his eyes scanning the crowds and his heart pounding with anticipation. He entered a restaurant with a bar and walked to the counter. He had learned that the bartenders could be helpful with information about their patrons. He sat down by the bar and gestured to the bartender. "Could you help me? I'm looking for a woman with dark hair, and she recently settled here and bought some mansions in this area."

"Do you have a name?" the bartender asked. He was a skinny man with an apron in front.

"I only know her as Miss Joliette. I don't know her last name." Henri confessed, realizing he had never learnt what her family name was. It would have made the search easier.

"I believe I know who you're looking for. She owns large mansions on the other side of the city. You can't miss them. They are the largest ones on King Street." He wiped the counter and added, "That lady has money. She never goes out alone, always with her trusted escorts."

Henri realized Joliette's vast fortune had elevated her to a prominent position in New Orleans' high society. She was a newcomer who had swiftly made a name for herself by acquiring multiple properties throughout the city, solidifying her influence and reputation as a woman of considerable means and refinement.

"Thank you." Henri left a silver coin for the bartender and walked outside. The air was balmy as he headed toward King Street.

When he finally got there, he immediately saw a few grand mansions that would fit the style a French woman would love. He chose to enter the first one. Henri crossed the front garden and arrived at the front, his footsteps echoing on the porch as he approached the entrance door.

A figure emerged from the shadows, her raven hair cascading down her back like a waterfall of night. Joliette's eyes gleamed with a knowing light as she embraced Henri, her touch warm and inviting.

"Welcome, *mon ami*," she whispered. "I've been expecting you. We have much to discuss and little time to waste."

Chapter Fifty-Two

Henri and Joliette

H enri stepped inside, feeling the nearness of her, the sameness, the strength, the attractiveness, and his knees buckled. He had found her. Everything was going to be all right.

As the door closed behind him, Henri's heart ached with the uncertainty of whether he would ever be reunited with his baby daughter. The distance between them seemed insurmountable.

As Henri trailed behind Joliette, he found himself ensconced in the opulent dining room, his gaze wandering to the splendid chandeliers that cast a kaleidoscope of crystal droplets across the walls. The room was a masterpiece of elegance, with oil paintings of ancestors past gazing down from the walls. Joliette must have brought all this with her. She had more time to prepare for her departure from Paris, Henri realized.

The air was heavy with the scent of old money and forgotten memories, and Henri's footsteps echoed on the hallway's hardwood floor following Joliette's slim figure. When Joliette sat down in a plush armchair, Henri knelt beside her, his shoulder touching her arm, wanting to be close to his creator, and he was happy in the midst of her heartbreak about Adele and their abducted daughter.

Joliette's sharp eyes studied him. "Something has changed."

"My whole world is gone. Everything has changed." His voice was quiet.

"Tell me." Joliette leaned back, never taking her eyes off of Henri's.

And Henri told her about his journey, how he met Adele and her pregnancy. The last part made Joliette raise her eyebrows, but she didn't comment but listened keenly.

When Henri got to the part where Adele was attacked and killed brutally, Joliette's eyes flashed with anger. Her hand gripped Henri's arms as he finished his story, "They cut off my unborn child from her dying mother, and I couldn't do anything but listen. The daylight burnt like I was in hell." Henri lowered his head against the armrest, and Joliette placed her hand over his head.

"You couldn't have done anything to change the course of events," she said softly, her hand moving in gentle strokes through his dark hair as she pondered the situation. "You truly believe your child is still alive?"

Henri lifted his head, meeting Joliette's gaze, and nodded. "Yes, I'm certain of it. She grew at an incredible rate, far faster than any ordinary human child. And then I discovered the truth: the Baudelaires are a family of werewolves. I learned about their secret from the villagers, but I couldn't muster the courage to confront them alone, unaware of what dangers lay within their mansion." Henri was painfully aware of how weak he sounded. "I wanted to save my child, but not at all costs. If the werewolves had seen me coming, they would have killed me one way or another, and they could have killed my daughter too."

"I need to think about this," Joliette replied looking pensive. "I'm curious about your daughter. You said she's your child, but the mother was a human. A rarity, that's what she is. I have to read some old books to find out what she is. I've never met a child born from a vampire. It's fascinating, and thus, she's worth saving from the claws of the werewolves." She stood up. "Rest now. I must convey this to our coven and the leaders of other vampire covens in this area. I will know more later."

"Thank you, Joliette."

She pulled a sash string, and while they waited for a servant enter the room she commented, "Our coven arrived here a while back. Almost all survived the journey. I only lost two during the storm. They couldn't stay below the deck because of the seasickness and wandered to the deck during the daytime. Their death was ... saddening, but we always knew the voyage was dangerous."

appeared by the doorway. "Take Monsieur Henri to one of my guestrooms, Jean."

Jean nodded in understanding. Henri's vampire nature suddenly struck him, and his thirst for blood surged.

Joliette's gaze swept the room, her voice dripping with subtle suggestion. "And, Jean, do see that some willing ladies join Henri in his chambers. I'm sure he would appreciate the... company."

With a graceful bow, Jean gestured for Henri to follow him to his quarters. "I'll ensure the servant girl prepares a bath for you, Henri. You must be exhausted."

As they entered the lavish bedroom, adorned with silk drapes and a grand double bed, Henri sank onto the plush surface, his weariness and grime suddenly overwhelming him.

It didn't take long before the servant girl arrived. She filled the ornate tub with warm, fragrant water, and Henri sank into its soothing depths, feeling the grime and fatigue of his journey melting away. The bath was a luxurious escape, scented with lavender and rose petals, and Henri closed his eyes, letting the warmth seep into his bones. Sighing, he closed his eyes and dozed off. He did not know how long he had enjoyed the luxury of the bath, but the servant girl wake him up and helped him in a silk morning robe and gestured for him to go lay down.

Later, as he lay on the silk-covered bed, two women entered the room, their eyes gleaming with a knowing light. They were beautiful and alluring, their skin smooth and unblemished, their full lips curved into inviting smiles. They moved with a sultry grace, their movements almost feline, as they approached Henri with an unmistakable intent. Their eyes seemed to gleam with desire, a hunger to satiate Henri's thirst, to quench the burning thirst awakened within him. They were the willing ladies Joliette had promised, and they came to Henri with open arms, ready to satisfy his thirst for human blood and indulge his deepest d esires.

After the two ladies left him, Henri lay awake the rest of the night struggling to understand his new surroundings, Juliette's fashionable home, and what she had told him: there was more than one vampire coven in New Orleans. When the sun rose, Henri fell into a restless slumber, having nightmares of her bellowed Adele and their daughter.

Henri's soul refused to surrender to the darkness, holding fast to the hope that one day, he would be granted the joy of embracing his child once more. He held on to the hope of a future reunion. Until that day, his heart would remain forever hers, a love that would bridge even the widest of distances.

Chapter Fifty-Three

Joliette's Decision

While Henri was taking a bath and quenching his thirst, Joliette had left the mansion and headed to the secret place in the middle of the woods where the vampire covens met.

Joliette's heels clicked against the stone slab floor as she entered the covens' hideout. She had learned how to navigate the treacherous landscape of vampire politics, her beauty and cunning the only weapons

she needed. All the other cover leaders were powerful, rich, and ancient vampires. She glided from one
shadowy salon to the next, leaving a trail of whispered
promises and veiled threats in her wake. The leaders of
the other covens listened intently, their eyes gleaming
with a calculating light, as Joliette explained what she
had learned from Henri and the werewolves.

"We won't and can't go against the Baudelaires,"
Anthon Fauver replied.

The weight of Anthon Fauver's words hung in the
air like a death sentence, his tone as unyielding as the
stone walls of his ancient mansion. His piercing gaze
bore into Joliette's very soul, leaving no doubt that
his decision was final. As the most powerful vampire in New Orleans, his influence was unparalleled,
his authority unchallenged. Joliette's eyes narrowed,
her mind racing with the implications of his denial.
Without Fauver's backing, their quest to rescue Henri's daughter was doomed from the start. His words
suffocated any previous words of possible support.
Joliette knew that.

Anthon kept his gaze on Joliette when he added, "The Baudelaires are powerful shifters, and they consider themselves to be better than any other shifters, even better than vampires." Anthon's eyes were light blue, set under straight thick white brows, which matched with his pale hair. "Besides, from time to time, we have used them in our business deals, and thus, I don't want to upset our business partners."

His refusal to support their cause was a crushing blow, reminding Joliette that in vampire politics, allegiances were forged and broken with caution.

As her eyes scanned the room, Joliette saw agreeing nods and heard murmuring, "Yes, we need them. They can do business in daylight whereas we can't. They understand the shifter world because they are part of it like we are."

The covens were wary of getting entangled in the affairs of the Baudelaires, Joliette understood.

When Joliette returned to Henri, her expression a mask of elegance and disappointment. She didn't go to his room but went to rest for the daytime.

Only when the horizon was set aflame with the fiery hues of sunset, painting the sky with vibrant shades of crimson and gold, did she summon Henri.

He was now dressed in a fine suit with a gold decorated vest left in his room. As he entered the living room, his heart was filled with hope that soon vanished when he heard Joliette's news.

"I'm afraid I have grave news, Henri," she said, her voice dripping with regret. "The other covens have declined our request for aid. They will not risk their own necks and their business deals to rescue your daughter from the Baudelaires." Her eyes locked onto his, and for a fleeting moment, Henri glimpsed the hint of genuine sorrow behind her gaze. "I'm afraid you will have to face this challenge alone... if you decide to do anything."

Henri's hands trembled as he ran them through his hair, his eyes wild with desperation. "How can I abandon her? She's not one of them, not a monster like the rest!"

Joliette's voice was calm and reassuring. "She may not be a vampire, Henri, but she's not entirely human either. She's a dhampir, a being with a unique heritage."

Henri's expression was one of stunned disbelief. "A dhampir? What does that even mean?"

Joliette's words were laced with conviction. "It means she'll possess extraordinary gifts, Henri. She'll live for centuries, walk in the sunlight, and possess strength beyond that of mortals. These qualities will be her armor, her shield against the werewolves that surround her. And I promise you, Henri, one day you will be reunited with your daughter. Have faith."

Henri's heart remained heavy with the weight of this news. He knew that he had to leave his daughter behind, trusting in the promise of their future reunion.

"Stay with me, Henri," Joliette begged standing up and walking toward him. "Don't start a war with the werewolves alone. I promise you times will change, and you will see your daughter."

Reluctantly, Henri bowed his head. His mind reeled with chaotic, fragments of memories and fears: the imminent death in Bastille, Joliette as a bat transforming him into a vampire, the never-ending desperate blood hunger of the vampires, the looming shadows in his old estate, Adele... sweet Adele, and then her horrible death, her endless screams, the pooled blood on the road, the missing child, and then the silence of the night. He had to put all those memories away and start his life again. He had no choice. Joliette was his creator, the leader of his vampire coven, and he had come for her advice. This was it. Crushed, heartbroken, took a deep breath. "I understand. I will d o as you say."

Joliette's gaze locked onto Henri's, her voice barely above a whisper. "I'll introduce you to the other covens, and you'll reunite with our Parisian kin." Her hand on his arm tightened. "But be prepared, Henri.

Alliances are shifting, and ancient rivalries simmer beneath the surface."

Henri's jaw clenched, his eyes burning with determination. "I won't abandon my child to the werewolves. She deserves to know her heritage, her mother's story... and her father's love." His voice dropped to a growl. "I'll claim her, no matter the cost."

Joliette's expression turned grave. "Tread carefully, Henri. The werewolves won't relinquish their prize easily. War looms on the horizon, and our covens are not united."

Henri's eyes flashed with a hint of steel. "I'll navigate the shadows, but I won't back down. For my daughter, I'll risk everything." The darkness in his gaze seemed to spread, like a promise – or a warning...

The Next in Series

These next books will continue the series:
Bloodlines of Reclamation and Bloodlines of Resur-
gence

About the Author

S he is a multi-genre author hailing from the picturesque landscapes of Finland, now making waves in the literary world from the tranquil shores of Michigan. With a penchant for exploring diverse genres, the author captivates readers with tales that traverse the realms of mystery, romance, thriller, sci-fi, and fantasy, weaving intricate narratives that transport audiences to worlds both familiar and fantastical. When not penning captivating stories, the author enjoys gardening and painting.

Also By The Author

I have several pennames based on genres, and all
my books are listed here:

The Starbound Orphans Series: (YA/Sci-Fi)

Starbound Orphans

Starbound Journey

Starbound Hearts

The Galactic Emperor (coming soon)

The Ackley Family Saga:

Lord Ackley's Choice

A Rose So Red

Court of Kisses

A Romance Short story:

Snowbound Strangers

Jaxon Axis -series (Dystopian, Sci-Fi):

Jaxon Axis and the First Crime

Jaxon Axis and the Ice Age

The Lost Tomb -series:

The Lost Tomb

Venomous Dunes

The Lost Oasis of Love

Mummy Returns

Wonderland series:

The Red Queen Executioner

The Otis Thorne Thriller series:

Fathers and Sons

Black Dust

The Facility

Death Walks in Washington D.C.

The Ashburn -series

On Death's Door

Finders Keepers

The Kingdom Series (fantasy, romantasy, YA)

Wings of Sea

Wings of War

Wings and Fins

Wings of Shadows

Westerns

The Lady and The Stubborn Rancher

The Lady and The Robber Baron

Bury My Dreams

The Cupid and the Elf -series:

Love Trap

Naughty Elf

Ghost Stories

Cursed Banshee

Don't Go There

The Boy Called Pink

Sci-Fi

The Host

Romantasy

Grimhilde

Titanic Paranormal Novel

Chasing Death

Middle Grade / Children's books:

Attack Of the Iguana

Evil Elves

Attack On the North Pole

Krampus Escapes

The Bad Boy Krampus

The Underground Cat Academy

Three Ghost Brothers (by A. T. Sorsa)

The Minotaur series:

Minotaur's Muse

Minotaur's Curse

Ariadne's Revenge

Ayla Jones (Dark, Gothic Romance, Paranormal romance, Romantasy)

Donder – the Claus Club series

No Way But Down – Book #1 of the Dragon Prophecy Series

Dragon Unleashed– Book #2 of the Dragon Prophecy Series

The Night Riders

Bloodlines of Revolution – Book #1 of Bloodlines series

Bobbie Robins Contemporary thrillers

Samantha Raven Trilogy:

I'll Be Your Shadow

I'll Never Let You Go

I'll Be Back

Anthologies:

The Tales of Howloween

Find a full list of serial fiction, novels:

https://beacons.ai/arlajonesbooks

Tiktok: @jonesesbooks and @authorarlajones

Facebook: www.facebook.com/authorarlajones

Instagram: https://www.instagram.com/arlajonesb

ooks

Serial Fiction Sites:

patreon.com/arlajones

ttps://getinkspired.com/en/u/authorarlajon

es/

ttps://reamstories.com/authorbobbierobins

ttps://reamstories.com/authorarlajones

ttps://reamstories.com/authoraylajones

Milton Keynes UK
Ingram Content Group UK Ltd.
UKHW022017071224
452128UK00001B/25

9 798230 575832